POOR PEOPLE
AND
A LITTLE HERO

Fyodor Dostoevsky

POOR PEOPLE

AND

A LITTLE HERO

Translated, with an Introduction, by
DAVID MAGARSHACK

ANCHOR BOOKS
DOUBLEDAY & COMPANY, INC.
GARDEN CITY, NEW YORK

The Anchor Book edition is the first publication
of *Poor People* and *A Little Hero*

Anchor Books edition: 1968

LIBRARY OF CONGRESS CATALOG CARD NUMBER 68–10605

CONTENTS

INTRODUCTION

The two stories in this volume, *Poor People* and *A Little Hero*, were the first and the last stories Dostoevsky wrote during the five years of his literary work before his exile and imprisonment in Siberia.

Poor People made Dostoevsky famous literally overnight. At the age of twenty-four he became a celebrity. Dmitry Grigorovich, a young writer who shared lodgings with Dostoevsky, showed the novel to the young poet Nikolai Nekrasov, who was planning to publish a symposium by different authors. The novel produced so tremendous an effect on Nekrasov that he took it to Visarion Belinsky, the most influential critic of that time, who immediately recognized that he was dealing with a writer of genius. Belinsky singled out the three features that were most characteristic of Dostoevsky's art: the truthfulness of descriptions of the everyday life of his heroes, the masterly delineation of character and social conditions and the profound perception of the tragic elements of life. The critic, nevertheless, constantly drew Dostoevsky's attention to the need for acquiring literary expertise, because he could not apparently get used to Dostoevsky's diffuse style and ascribed it to the inexperience of a young writer. But he was mistaken. He did not realise that he was not dealing with a literary tyro, but with a full-fledged writer whose working methods had become set. Dostoevsky listened to the critic's admonitions with an air of benevolent indifference. The sudden success of his novel did more than free him from the doubts and hesitations which usually beset the first steps of a writer: he accepted it as a prophetic dream holding out the promise of future fame.

Dostoevsky's first novel, which was published in Nekrasov's *Petersburg Symposium* on January 15, 1846, was responsible for the literary term "the natural school" of Russian fiction popularised by Belinsky. Describing Devushkin's reaction to Pushkin's story *The Station Master*, Dostoevsky wrote: "I nearly burst into tears when I read that the poor fellow took to drink, lost his memory, became embittered and took to . . . sleeping all day long under a sheepskin, crying bitterly, wiping his eyes with the dirty skirt of his coat as he thought of his stray lamb, his daughter Dunyasha. Yes, that is natural! Read it—it is natural! It lives! I have seen it myself—it's happening all around me." Belinsky took his term of "the natural school" from this passage in Dostoevsky's story, enlarging it to mean not only the realistic movement in Russian literature, but also one that is conscious of the social and political iniquities of the tsarist *régime*.

After breaking with Belinsky, Dostoevsky became a member of a group of radicals headed by Mikhail Butashevich-Petrashevsky, a young and very rich political dilettante and an enthusiastic follower of the French utopian Socialist, Charles Fourier. He was often to be found at Petrashevsky's Friday at-homes, at which politics was the main topic of discussion. At one of them Dostoevsky read Belinsky's famous letter to Gogol in which the Russian critic attacked the reactionary opinions expressed by Gogol in his *Correspondence with Friends*.

Dostoevsky was arrested with the other members of the Petrashevsky "group" on April 23, 1849. He was imprisoned for eight months in the Peter and Paul Fortress in Petersburg and then sentenced to death, a sentence which was commuted to eight years' imprisonment in Siberia.

Dostoevsky broke with his liberal past during his imprisonment in Siberia, but the signs of the coming change can already be discerned in *A Little Hero*, intended as a children's story and written during his solitary confinement in the Peter and Paul Fortress. In this story Dostoevsky draws an amazingly frank picture of Petrashevsky in the guise of the husband of Mrs. M——, as a man with "a lump of fat instead of a heart."

A Little Hero is not only remarkable for Dostoevsky's fine analysis of the mentality of an eleven-year-old boy but also unique for its deeply sympathetic characterisation of an erring wife, the young married woman, Mrs. M——, with whom the young boy falls in love.

On July 18, 1849, Dostoevsky wrote to his brother from the fortress: "I have not wasted my time: I have jotted down the plots of three stories and two novels. One of them I am writing now." Only one of these stories, *A Little Hero*, first entitled *A Children's Fairytale*, has survived.

The first story by Dostoevsky to appear in print for eight years, it was published anonymously by Dostoevsky's elder brother in August, 1857, in the Petersburg monthly *Home Annals*. The news of its publication greatly displeased Dostoevsky. "I have been thinking of revising it," he wrote to his brother, "and first of all throw out everything that is bad, but it is too late now." The opportunity for revision came with the publication of his complete works in 1860. He cut out the introduction—a sentimental dedication to a certain Mashenka, for whom the author was supposed to have written the story—as well as the many invocations to Mashenka in the text.

Dostoevsky introduces children in many of his novels, most of them victims of evil social conditions who never experience the joys of childhood. The boy in *A Little Hero*, however, is quite different from any other children in Dostoevsky's stories and novels. He is, for one thing, remarkably receptive to the beauties of nature, a theme one does not usually associate with Dostoevsky. He is also receptive to every nuance of the emotional tragedy of the story's heroine, to whom he is attracted by a force that bewilders and baffles him, a force that fills him with "the blank misgivings of a creature moving about in worlds not realised." This romantic love of a boy for a grown-up woman, which is so completely devoid of egoism, is something Dostoevsky never attempted to describe before or after his Siberian imprisonment. It reveals the strong romantic streak in Dostoevsky's nature which derives not from Wordsworth (with the sole exception of Byron, the English romantic movement exerted no influence on Russian nineteenth-century literature), but from Schiller and from Dostoevsky's admiration for Schiller's heroes de Lorge and Togenburg, mentioned in the story, an admiration that persisted to the very end, as becomes all too clear from *The Brothers Karamazov*. The knight-errantry motif, incidentally, occurs once again in *The Idiot*, though in an entirely different context.

D.M.

POOR PEOPLE

A NOVEL

Oh, those story-tellers! They are not content to write something useful, pleasant, enjoyable, but dig up every unsavoury fact about their characters! I'd have forbidden them to write! I mean, think of it. . . . You read and . . . you cannot help wondering, and before you know, your head is full of all sorts of ridiculous ideas. I really would forbid them to write. Yes, indeed, simply forbid them to write.

Prince V. F. Odoevsky.

April 8th.

My precious Barbara,

Oh, I was so happy last night, so terribly, so marvellously happy! You had listened to me for once in your life, you stubborn darling. Last evening, about eight o'clock, I woke up (you know, dear heart, that I enjoy a short nap of about an hour after coming home from the office), I lit a candle, got my papers ready, trimmed my pen, then, suddenly, chanced to raise my eyes—and, I promise you, my heart leapt with joy! So you did understand what I wanted you to do so badly, what my poor heart was so longing for! I saw a corner of the curtain of your window was turned up and fixed

to your flower-pot of balsam, exactly as I had suggested to you the other day. I also thought that I
caught a glimpse of your dear face at the window, that
you, too, were looking at me from your room; that you,
too, were thinking of me. I was so sorry, my darling,
that I was not able to make out your sweet face clearly
enough. There was a time, dear heart, when I could
see things well enough. But, my dear, old age is no
joy. Now, too, everything seems to go blurred before
my eyes. I have only to do a little work at night, do
a bit of writing, and in the morning my eyes are bloodshot and start watering so that I can't help feeling
ashamed in public. But in my mind's eye I could see
your bright smile, my angel, and my heart was full of
the same feeling as when I kissed you that day, dear
Barbara—do you remember? You know, my darling, I
even seem to remember that you wagged your finger
at me that time, didn't you, you naughty girl? You
simply must describe it to me in detail in your next
letter.

Well, and what about that clever idea of yours about
the curtain, dear Barbara? Such a lovely idea, isn't it?
Every time I sit down to do some work, or am going to
bed, or waking up, I know that you are well and
happy. When you lower your curtain, well, it's "Good-
night, Mr. Devushkin. It's time I went to bed." When
you raise it— "Good morning, Mr. D., have you slept
well?" Or, "how are you this morning, Mr. D.?" As for
me, I am, thank God, very well. So you see, my darling,
how cleverly it was planned. No need for letters! Cunning, isn't it? So, you see how clever I am in such
matters, my dear Miss Dobroselov.

Let me tell you, dear heart, that I slept soundly last

night, against all my expectations, I am happy to say, although, as a rule, one does not sleep well in new lodgings because one is not used to new surroundings. Everything seems to be the same and yet not quite the same. I got up this morning very early—dawn was just breaking—it was lovely! What a joyous morning it was, dear heart! I opened my window: the sun was shining, the birds were twittering, the air was full of the scents of spring and all nature was coming to life, and, well, everything else also was in accordance with it. Why, I even indulged in some rather pleasant dreams today, and all my dreams were about you, my dear. I compared you to a bird created for the delight of men and for an adornment of nature. And then I could not help thinking, my dear, that we, people who live a life of cares and tribulations, should also envy this carefree and innocent happiness of the birds of heaven, and, well, more of the same kind. . . . I mean, I kept making such extravagant comparisons. You see, my dear, I have a book which has the same kind of thing in it. It describes all in great detail. I'm saying this, dear heart, because there are all sorts of dreams. And since it is spring now, my thoughts, too, are all so pleasant, so stimulating and fanciful, and my reveries are so soft-hued, everything rose-tinted. That is why I have written all this. Anyway, I got it all out of that book of mine. Its author reveals the same sort of desires in verse. He writes:

Why am I not a bird, a bird of prey?
And so on. All sorts of other thoughts find expression there, but enough of that! But where were you off to this morning, my dear? I was not ready to go to the office, when you, like a true bird in springtime, flut-

tered out of your room and walked across the courtyard looking so gay. I, too, felt gay watching you. Oh,
my dear, my dear Barbara, don't ever give way to
grief! Tears are no remedy against grief. I know that,
dear heart, I learned that from experience. Besides, you
are so contented now, and your health, too, has improved a little. Well, how is your Theodora? What a
kind woman she is! You must write to me, my dear,
about how you are getting on with her and whether
you are satisfied with everything. Theodora, it is true,
is a little grumpy, but you mustn't mind that. Let her
be. She is such a good soul.

I have already told you about our Teresa—another
good and reliable woman. I was so worried about our
letters, you see. How were they to be delivered? And,
then, God sent us Teresa. She is a good-natured
woman, gentle and meek. But our landlady is a real
tartar of a woman. Treats her like a door mat.

Oh, my dear, what a horrible slum I have got myself into! What lodgings! Before, as you know, I used
to live quietly, like an anchorite: peace and quiet; if
a fly flew across my room, I could hear it. But here—
noise, shouts, screams! Why, you have no idea what
things are like here. Imagine a long corridor, dark and
filthy. On the right is a blank wall, on the left a long
row of doors just as if it were an hotel. These rooms
are let—a little room and two or three people in a
room. Don't ask how it is all arranged—a veritable
Noah's Ark. Still, the people seem to be decent
enough, all well-educated and even erudite. One of
them is a civil servant (he has a job in the literary
section of some department), a well-read man: dis-
courses on Homer and Brambeus and all sorts of other

writers, on anything, in fact—an intelligent man.
There are also a couple of army officers who spend
all their time playing cards. Also a midshipman, and
an Englishman—a tutor. But I'll describe them to you
in my next letter—it will amuse you—satirically, I
mean, what they are really like, in great detail. Our
landlady is a very little woman, and very dirty, who
walks about in slippers and a dressing gown all day and
is always shouting at Teresa. I, myself, live in the
kitchen, or, to put it more correctly, in a room next
to the kitchen (our kitchen, I must tell you, is very
bright and clean), a rather small room—a modest little
nook of a place—or, to put it more plainly, the kitchen
is very large with three windows and it has a partition
running along the opposite wall, and I live behind it
in a sort of supernumerary apartment. There is plenty
of room, it is comfortable, and I even have a window;
in short, it's adequate. Well, that's my little place.
But, please, do not imagine, dear heart, that there's
some mystery about it, some secret. I mean, that it is,
after all, a kitchen. Well, I do, as a matter of fact,
live in the same room behind a partition, but that's
nothing. I live by myself, alone, apart from everybody.
I live quietly, without fuss. I have put in a bed, a table,
a chest of drawers and a couple of chairs. Hung up an
icon. There are, of course, better rooms, but comfort is,
after all, the main thing. You see, I have done it all for
the sake of convenience, and please do not imagine
that it was for anything else. Your window is just
opposite across the yard, and the yard being so narrow
I can see you now and then—this makes me feel better,
poor wretch that I am, and it's cheaper, too. In this
house the cheapest room with board costs thirty-five

roubles. It's more than I can afford. But my room costs only seven roubles in paper money and for the board five silver roubles, making in all twenty-four and a half roubles in paper money, while before I used to pay thirty roubles and so had to deny myself many things. I had to do without tea sometimes, but now I can afford both tea and sugar. You see, my dear, I feel it's rather humiliating to have to do without tea, for everyone here is well-to-do and one can't help feeling humiliated. I drink tea because the others do, Barbara, my dear, for appearance's sake—not to let the place down. I don't mind myself, I'm not particular myself. Now, I must have some money, don't you think? I mean for a pair of boots, for clothes. How much of it will remain? That's all my salary gone. I'm not grumbling. I'm satisfied. It's sufficient. It's been sufficient for some years. And there are all sorts of bonuses. Well, good-bye, my angel. I've bought two little pots of balsam and a geranium for you—very cheap. Do you also like mignonette by any chance? I've some mignonette, too. Write to me. And, please, do write in more detail. Don't imagine anything, dear heart, I mean about my renting this room. Don't worry about it. It was solely a question of convenience. I've been tempted by the thought of convenience. You see, dear heart, I'm saving up, putting money aside. I've plenty of money. Don't be deceived by my appearing to be such a harmless old codger who might be hurt by the wing of a fly. No, dear heart, I know how to look after myself and I can say that my character is such as becomes a man who possesses a firm and untroubled nature. Good-bye, my sweet angel. I have covered almost two sheets of paper, and it's high time I went to the office.

I kiss your sweet little fingers, dear heart, and remain
                    Your most humble and faithful friend,
                                    Makar Devushkin.

P.S. One thing I must ask you: please answer this
letter, my angel, as fully as possible. I send you a box
of sweets with this letter, dearest Barbara. I hope you
like them, and for goodness' sake do not worry about
me and do not be angry with me. Well, good-bye
again, dear heart.

                                        April 8th.

Dear Mr. Devushkin,

I'm afraid I really shall be angry with you in good
earnest. Why, my dear, kind Mr. Devushkin, I simply
cannot accept your presents. I know how much they
must have cost you, what privations you must have suffered on my account, and how many things you must
have denied yourself. I want nothing, absolutely nothing. How many times have I told you that I cannot
repay you for the things you have so generously show-
ered on me. What do I need more flower-pots for? I
don't mind the balsam, but why send me the geraniums? I happen to let slip a word, as, for instance, about
those geraniums, and off you go and buy me some! I
expect you paid a lot for them. Oh, they are so lovely
with their scarlet petals! Where did you get such beautiful geraniums? I have put them in the middle of my
window, in the most conspicuous place! I'm going to
put a bench on the floor and more flowers on the
bench—let me only get enough money first! Theodora
is so pleased! My room is just like paradise—so bright
and clean. But why the sweets? You see, I guessed at
once from your letter that things were not so well with

you—it is a little too full of paradise and spring and fragrance and the twittering of birds. Why, I said to myself, aren't there any poems, too? Indeed, dear Mr. Devushkin, the only thing your letter lacks is poetry. Such tender feelings, such rose-coloured fancies! There is everything there. As for the curtain—I never thought of it. I expect it must have got caught on to the flower-pots when I moved them. So there!

My dear Mr. Devushkin, whatever you say and whatever you may make out your income to be to deceive me and make me feel that you spend it all on yourself, you cannot conceal or hide anything from me. I can see that you are denying yourself because of me. What on earth made you take such a room, for instance? You are certainly troubled and disturbed, aren't you? You haven't enough elbow room. You're uncomfortable. You love solitude, and here everything is on top of you. You could have lived very much better on your salary. Theodora tells me that you've lived much better than you do now. Have you really spent all your life in solitude and want, without joy, without a friendly word, renting some corner of a room from total strangers? My dear friend, I feel so sorry for you. At least take good care of your health, dear Mr. Devushkin. You say your eyesight is failing, so please don't go and write by candlelight. Why do you? Your superiors, I am sure, are well aware of your zeal, as it is!

Once more, I implore you, do not spend too much money on me. I know you love me, but you're not a rich man, are you? . . . I, too, got up this morning feeling on top of the world. I was so happy: Theodora

had long been at work and she had found work for
me too. I was so glad, I only went out for some silk
and sat down to work. All morning I felt so light-
hearted, so cheerful. But now, again, I feel terribly
depressed, miserable and sick at heart.

Oh dear, what's going to become of me? What sort
of prospects can I hope for? What's so unbearable is
that I don't know what's going to happen to me. I'm
terrified to look back on my past. It is so full of sorrow
that my heart breaks at the very thought of it. All my
life I shall execrate the wicked people who ruined my
life.

It is getting dark. Time I did some work. I'd have
liked to write much more to you, but I have no time.
My work must be finished tonight. I must hurry.
Of course, I like writing letters: it helps to while away
the time. But why don't you ever come to see me?
Why not, dear Mr. Devushkin? You don't live too far
now, do you? And you do have some free time sometimes, don't you? Do come, please. I've seen your
Teresa. She looks so ill. I felt so sorry for her, I gave
her twenty copecks. Goodness, I nearly forgot! Please,
write to me all about yourself. What the people are
like in your house, and are you getting on well with
them? I'd very much like to know all about it. Write
without fail, please. I shall most certainly hitch up the
curtain tonight. Go to bed early. Last night I could
see a light burning in your room until midnight. Well,
good-bye. I feel so depressed, sad and weary tonight.
I suppose it's one of those days. Good-bye.

Yours,

B. Dobroselov.

April 8th.

My dear Miss Dobroselov,

Yes, dear heart, yes, indeed, my darling, it was one of those days, poor wretch that I am! Yes, you certainly pulled my leg, an old man like me! But it's my own fault. I am to blame for it all. A man of my advanced years, with only a tuft of hair on his head, should not let himself be involved in love affairs and in all sorts of equivocal situations. And let me add, dear heart, man is a funny creature. Heavens above, the things he will say, the nonsense he will talk sometimes! And what's the result? What follows? Why, nothing follows, except the sort of mess that the good Lord preserve us from! Mind you, I am not in the least angry, dear heart. I merely feel very sorry to recall it all, sorry to have written such a stupid and flowery letter to you. And you should have seen me strutting off to the office today—a regular dandy! My heart was full of sunshine. I was in a real holiday mood for some reason: happy as a sandboy I was. I threw myself upon my work with great zeal—but with what result? When I looked round later, everything was just as before—dull and gloomy. The same inkstains, the same tables and documents, and I, too, was the same: I was exactly the same as I had been, so why go off on a ride on Pegasus? What was the reason for it all? Was it because the sun had peeped out and the sky was blue? Was that the reason? And what is all this about the fragrant air when, far from fragrant, things are all too often to be found in our courtyard under the windows? I must have dreamed it all up in a moment of aberration. For it does happen sometimes that a man gets so carried away by his own feelings that he

starts talking all sorts of nonsense. It is caused, I daresay, by some stupid excess of ardour in the heart. I did
not walk home but dragged myself there. My head
was aching for some reason. Trouble, it seems, never
comes singly. (I may have got a chill in my back.) You
see, fool that I am, so overjoyed was I at the spring
weather that I had gone out in my summer overcoat.
You were wrong about my feelings, too, my dear. You
completely misinterpreted them. I was carried away
by paternal feelings, solely by paternal feelings, my
dear. Poor orphan that you are, I regard myself simply
as your father. I say this in all sincerity, out of the
purity of my heart, as a relative of yours. For though
I may be a distant relative, a second cousin twice removed, I am a relative still, for when you had the
right to look for help and protection, you found only
treachery and insults. As for poetry, let me tell you,
dear heart, that it ill becomes me in my old age to
waste time in writing poems. Poetry is stuff and nonsense! Even boys are now whipped at school for writing poems—that is how it is, my dear.

Why, my dear, are you writing to me about comfort, peace and so on? Dear heart, I am not a fastidious
or demanding person, and I never lived better than
I do now. So why should I be hard to please in my
old age? I have enough to eat, I am decently dressed
and shod. Besides, who am I to get all sorts of fanciful ideas? I am not of noble descent. My father was
no nobleman and he and his large family were much
worse off than I. Neither am I effeminate. However,
if I am to tell the truth, my lodgings were infinitely
better. There was much more space there, dear heart.
No doubt, my present ones are quite good and even

more cheerful in some respects, and, if you like, less monotonous. I have nothing to say against this room, but I can't help missing my old lodgings. We old men, I mean, elderly men, get used to old things just as if they were something near and dear to us. My old room, you know, was such a nice little place; the walls —well, the walls were just like any other walls—they don't matter; it's just that the memory of my past life makes me feel depressed. It's a funny thing. It is not as if my past life was a bed of roses, but my memories of it seem to be pleasant. Even the bad things, the things that used to vex me, seem to be washed clean in my memory and appear in an attractive light in my imagination. We used to live there quietly, my dear, my landlady, who is now dead, and I. I can't help feeling sad every time I remember the dear old lady. She was a good woman, and she did not charge me a great deal for my room. She used to spend all her time making patchwork blankets with knitting needles a yard long. It was the only work she did. We used to share the same candle, she and I, working at one table together. She had a grand-daughter, Masha—I remember her as a baby—she'd be thirteen now. She was such a mischievous little thing, so merry, she amused us all. During the long winter evenings, we used to sit down at the round table, have tea, and then set to work. The old lady used to tell fairy-tales to amuse the child and to keep her out of mischief. Such wonderful fairy-tales they were, too! Not only a child, but a clever and intelligent man could not help listening to them. Why, I myself used to light my pipe and sit listening to them and forget my work. The child, too, a little bundle of mischief, would grow thoughtful, prop

her rosy cheek on her little hand, open her pretty
mouth, and the moment something fearful happened
in the story, she would cling closer—closer to the old
lady. It was a real treat to look at her. You didn't
notice the flickering candle and you didn't hear the
howling of the snowstorm outside. Oh, it was a good
life, my dear, and we lived like that for nearly twenty
years together. But I'm sorry, I've been talking too
much. I don't suppose you are even faintly interested
in such a subject, neither do I find it pleasant to recall
—especially at this twilight hour. Teresa is pottering
about in the kitchen. My head aches, and my back,
too, is aching a little. All sorts of queer ideas seem to
be coming into my head—as though they, too, are in
pain. I feel sad today, my dear. What do you mean,
my dear? How could I come to see you? My darling,
what will people say? I have only to cross the courtyard for the people in our lodgings to notice it, to
start asking questions. They'd start talking, spreading
scandalous stories, put quite a different interpretation
on the matter. No, my dear angel, I'd better see you
tomorrow at vespers. That would be much more sensible and less harmful to both of us. And please, do
not think badly of me for having written such a letter
to you. On rereading it, though, I can see that it is a
little incoherent. You see, my dear, I am an old man
of no education. I did not learn a lot when I was
young, and I'm afraid it's too late for me to start study-
ing again. I own, dear heart, that I'm not good at
describing things and I know, without anyone pointing it out to me or making fun of me, if I take it into
my head to write anything more or less entertaining,
I shall talk a lot of nonsense. . . . I saw you at your

today, I saw you drawing down the blind. Good-bye, good-bye, God bless you. Good-bye, my dear Barbara.

Your selfless friend,
Makar Devushkin.

P.S. I'm afraid, my dear, I do not write satires on anyone now. I'm too old, dear heart, to bare my teeth to no purpose. Besides, they'd only laugh at me. As the old saw had it: he who digs a pit for another man will fall into it himself.

April 9th.

Dear Mr. Devushkin,

You ought to be ashamed of yourself, my friend and benefactor, to get yourself into such a state and make such a fuss over nothing. You are not offended, are you? Oh dear, I'm often indiscreet, but I never thought that you would take any words as a satirical jest at your expense. I promise you I shall never make fun of your age or your character. It all happened because of my thoughtlessness, or rather, because I feel so terribly bored, and one does anything out of boredom. You see I was under the impression that you yourself wanted to have a good laugh in your letter. I was terribly upset when I realised that you were displeased with me. I'm sorry, my dear friend and benefactor, but you will be making a big mistake if you suspect me of ingratitude and lack of feeling. Deep down in my heart I know what to think of all you have done for me by protecting me from wicked people and their persecution and hatred. I shall pray for you all my life, and if my prayers ever reach God and Heaven heeds them, then, I'm sure, you will be happy.

I am not feeling too well today. I'm hot and shivery, in turn. Theodora is very worried about me. You mustn't be afraid of coming to see me, dear Mr. Devushkin. It's no concern of anybody's. You know me and that's all there is to it. . . . Good-bye, dear Mr. Devushkin. I have nothing more to write about and, besides, I'm feeling too unwell to write. I beg you again not to be angry with me and rest assured of my constant regard and of the attachment with which I have the honour to remain your most devoted and humble servant,

Barbara Dobroselov.

April 12th.

Dear Miss Dobroselov,

Goodness gracious, dear heart, what is the matter with you? Every time you fill me with alarm. In every letter I beg you to take care of yourself, to wrap yourself up warmly, not to go out in bad weather, not to run any risks, and you, my little angel, pay no heed to me. Goodness, my darling, you act as if you were a child! You're so weak, so terribly weak. A breath of wind, and you're ill. So you must take good care of yourself, look after yourself, avoid all risks, and not drive your friends into despondency and despair.

You have expressed a wish, dear heart, to learn all about my way of life and my surroundings. I am only too glad to satisfy that wish of yours, my dear. Let me begin from the beginning, dear heart: it will be more methodical that way. To begin with, the stairs leading from the main entrance are fair enough, particularly the main staircase which is light, clean and wide, all iron and mahogany. But the back stairs are terri-

ble: spiral, damp, dirty, the steps broken and the walls
so greasy that your hand sticks fast when you lean
against them. Each landing is cluttered up with
trunks, chairs and battered wardrobes; washing hanging on lines; windows broken; bins filled with all sorts
of filth, litter, eggshells and fish bladders; the stench
is horrible. . . . In a word, the place is a disgrace.

I have already described the disposition of the
rooms to you: it is convenient, no doubt, but the
rooms are stuffy; I do not mean that they smell badly,
but there is, if one may put it that way, a sort of rank,
sickly-sweet odour about them. At first sight the impression is unfavourable, but all that does not really
matter: after a moment or two it will disappear, and
you won't even be aware of its disappearance, for
somehow you become permeated with that smell yourself. Your hands, clothes, everything will become
soaked with it and—well, you get used to it. But
siskins just die here. Our midshipman has just bought
his fifth siskin but they don't live in our air; you can
do nothing about it. Our large kitchen is bright and
spacious. It is true that in the mornings it is full of
fumes when fish or beef is being fried, and, besides,
people spill water all over the floor, but in the evenings it's paradise. In the kitchen, washing—old linen
—is hanging on lines to dry; and since my room is not
far away, I mean, it practically adjoins the kitchen,
I am, I admit, a little bothered by the smell from the
washing. But it's of no great consequence. One gets
used to anything in life.

From very early morning, my dear, our home is a
hive of activity. People get up, walk up and down,
make a noise—all who have got to go to work—in some

government department or somewhere else. They get
out of bed and start having their breakfast. Most of
our samovars belong to our landlady and, as there
aren't many of them, we all have to queue up for our
tea. Anyone who tries to jump the queue, gets a
proper dressing down. The first time, I'm sorry to say,
I was the culprit and—well, why harp on it? It was
then that I struck up an acquaintance with them all.
First of all with our midshipman—very frank he was,
too. Told me about his father, his mother, his sister,
who is married to a Tula assessor, and about the city
of Kronstadt. He offered me his patronage and invited me to have tea with him. I found him in the
room where we usually play cards. I was offered a
cup of tea and forced to join in a game of cards. I
don't know whether they were just pulling my leg, but
they had certainly played all night through, and when
I came into the room, they were still playing. The
room was full of chalk, cards and smoke so that my
eyes began to smart. I declined to play and I was at
once told that I was talking like a philosopher. After
that no one spoke to me at all the whole time and, to
tell the truth, I was glad of it. I'm not going there
again—they're inveterate gamblers, the lot of them.
The official who has a job in some department dealing
with literature also gives parties in the evenings. But
at his place everything is nice, decent, innocent and
tactful—the height of refinement.

Well, my dear, let me tell you, by the way, that our
landlady is a most horrible woman, a veritable witch,
in fact. You have seen Teresa. Well, what do you think
of her? Thin, like a sickly, plucked chicken. There

are only two servants in this house: Teresa and
Faldoni, the landlady's servant. I don't know if Faldoni has another name, but he only answers to this
one: everyone calls him by it. He's red-haired, a Finn,
I suppose, blind in one eye, snubnosed, rude: wran-
gling with Teresa all the time, and they almost come
to blows. As a matter of fact, I don't find life altogether pleasant here. . . . To fall asleep at once and
have a good night's rest is something that never happens here. Somewhere people are always sitting down
to a game of cards. Sometimes something happens that
I would rather not talk about. I have got used to it all
by this time, but I still cannot help being surprised
how men with families can live in a Sodom like this.
A whole family of impecunious people have rented one
of our landlady's rooms apart from the other rooms,
at the other side of the flat, in a corner by itself. Quiet
people. One never hears a sound from them. They
live in one room, divided up by a partition. He seems
to be a civil servant out of a job, dismissed from the
service for something or other seven years ago. His
name is Gorshkov: a grey-haired little man, walks
about in such a greasy, threadbare coat, that it is
painful to see. Much worse than mine! A pitiful puny
creature (I run across him in the passage sometimes).
His knees knock together, his hands shake, his head
quivers with some disease—goodness only knows what.
He is very shy, afraid of everyone, walks along hugging
the wall. I am rather shy myself sometimes, but he is
much worse. His family consists of a wife and three
children. The eldest one—a boy—is the spitting image
of his father, as sickly as he. His wife must have been

quite good-looking, one can see that even now, but the poor woman walks about in awful rags. I understand they owe money to our landlady, who does not appear to be particularly well-disposed to them. I have also heard that Gorshkov lost his job because of some unpleasantness or other—I don't think any legal action has been taken against him, but his case is under investigation now—I don't really know for certain. They are terribly poor—good Lord, how poor! There is dead silence in their room, just as if no one lived there. Even the children cannot be heard. Indeed, I can't remember the children ever romping about or playing—and that's a bad sign. One evening when I happened to pass the door of their room at a time when it was quite unusually quiet in the house, I heard the sound of sobbing inside, then whispering, then sobbing again, just as if someone were weeping, but so quietly, so miserably that my heart nearly burst with pity. All night I kept thinking of those poor people— I could hardly sleep a wink.

Well, good-bye, my dear, dear friend, my darling Barbara. I have described everything to the best of my ability. Today I have been thinking of you all the time. My heart has been aching for you all day long. You see, my darling, I know that you have no warm coat. Oh, these frightful Petersburg springs—winds, rains, snow showers. I can't bear them myself, my dear. The Lord preserve me from such lovely weather! I am sorry, my dear, for the way I write. I'm afraid that I lack style. If only I had some kind of style. I put down everything that comes into my head so as to cheer you up a little. Of course if I had had some education, it would be different. But what sort of education did I have? Too poor to get even an elementary education.

Your ever faithful friend,
Makar Devushkin.

April 25th.

Dear Mr. Devushkin,

Today I met my cousin Sasha. How awful! She, too, will be ruined, poor thing! I have also learned, incidentally, that Anna Fyodorovna is still inquiring about me. I don't think she will ever stop persecuting me. She says she wants to forgive me, to forget the past and that she is quite determined to come and see me. She says that you are no relation of mine at all, that she is much more of a relation of mine, that you have no right to interfere in our family relationships, and that it is I who ought to be ashamed of myself to live upon your charity and to be kept by you. She says that I must have forgotten all she had done for me, that she saved my mother and myself from starvation, that she kept us, that she incurred considerable losses on our behalf, and that she has never asked us to repay the money we owed her. She did not spare even my mother. If my poor mother only knew what they did to me! God alone knows that! Anna Fyodorovna says that it was entirely my own fault that I failed to make use of the golden opportunity which she placed in my way, that she could not be blamed for what happened afterwards, that I myself was unable, or, perhaps, did not want to defend my honour. But whose fault was it, great God! She says Mr. Bykov was quite right and that one could not expect a man to marry a woman who—but what's the use of writing about it? It is cruel to hear such a lie, dear Mr. Devushkin! I don't know what's the matter with me just now. I shake all over and sob and weep. It took me two hours to write this letter. I thought that at least she realised how much he was to blame for what has happened to me. But that's how she is behaving now! Please, my friend, my only well-wisher, do not worry about me. Theodora always exaggerates. I am not ill. I merely caught a slight cold yesterday on my way to Volkhovo Cemetery to order a mass for the soul of my mother. Why didn't you come with me? I have asked you so often. Oh, poor, poor mother, if you could rise from the grave, if you knew, if you saw what they had done to me!

Barbara Dobroselov.

May 20th.

My darling Barbara,

I am sending you a few grapes, my darling. I am told they are good for convalescents, and the doctor, too, recommends them for quenching thirst, so they are just for quenching your thirst. You expressed a wish for roses the other day, dear heart, so I am sending you some. How is your appetite, my darling? That's the chief thing that matters. Still, thank God, it's all over and done with and our misfortunes are also coming to an end. Let me offer up thanks to heaven! As for books, I'm afraid I cannot get hold of them anywhere for the time being. I'm told there is one excellent book written in a lofty style. It is said to be an excellent book. I haven't read it myself, but it is highly praised here. I have asked for it myself and been lent it. Only are you going to read it? I know

you to be hard to please in this respect. It is difficult
to satisfy your taste. I know you too well, my darling.
I suppose all you want is poetry—amorous sighs, love
affairs—well, I'll get you poems, I'll get you everything.
I have some copied out in a book.

I am quite all right. Don't you worry about me, dear
heart. What Theodora told you about me is just a lot
of nonsense. You tell her it's just a pack of lies. Don't
fail to tell her that, the old gossip. I have not sold my
new civil service uniform. Judge for yourself: why
should I have sold it? I have been promised a bonus
of forty roubles in silver, so why should I have sold it?
Don't worry, dear heart. She is over-suspicious, Theodora. We're going to have a good time, my darling.
Only do get well, my little angel. You get well first, do
not grieve an old man. Who told you that I have lost
weight? A slander, another slander! I am in fine fettle
and have, in fact, put on weight—so much that I am
ashamed of myself. I am happy, contented. All I wish
is that you should get well. Good-bye, my angel. I kiss
all your dear fingers and remain

Your eternal, unfailing friend,
Makar Devushkin.

P.S. Dear me, my darling, what are you writing to me
again? What queer ideas are you getting into your
head? How could I come and visit you so often, dear
heart? How?—I ask you. Perhaps by taking advantage
of a dark night. Unfortunately, there are hardly any
dark nights now, not at this season. Why, dear heart,
my little angel, I scarcely left your side during your
illness, while you were unconscious. I simply don't
know how I managed to do all those things and only
stopped visiting you later because people were getting
curious and beginning to ask me questions. Even as it

was, people were beginning to talk. I put my trust in
Teresa: she doesn't talk too much. But, really, dear
heart, what is going to happen when they find out
everything about us? What will people think and what
will they be saying then? So, please, dear heart, have
patience and wait until you are well again, and then
we shall, somehow, arrange a rendezvous somewhere
outside.

June 1st.

Dearest Mr. Devushkin,

I am so anxious to do something to please and
amuse you in return for all the trouble I have caused
you, for all your love for me, that I have decided at
last, having nothing else to do, to rummage in my
chest of drawers and try to find my journal, which I
am sending off to you now. I began it during the happy
period of my life. You showed so much interest in my
former way of life and kept asking me so many questions about it, about my mother, about Pokrovsky,
about the time I spent with Anna Fyodorovna and,
finally, about my more recent misfortunes, and you
were so anxious to read the journal in which, goodness
only knows why, I took it into my head to record some
brief episode of my life, that I do not doubt to give
great pleasure by sending it to you. I felt a little sad
reading it again. I can't help feeling that I have grown
twice as old since I wrote the last line of my journal.
It was all written at different times. Good-bye, dear
Mr. Devushkin. I feel terribly weary now and I often
suffer from insomnia. Convalescence is such a terrible
bore!

Barbara Dobroselov.

1.

I was only fourteen when my father died. Childhood was the happiest time of my life. It did not begin here, but very far away from here, in the provinces, in the wilds of the country. My father was steward of the large estates of Prince P. in the Tula province. We lived on one of the Prince's estates, and lived a quiet, undisturbed, happy life. I was such a high-spirited little girl; all I did was run about the fields, the woods, the garden and no one ever took the slightest notice of me. My father was always occupied with his business affairs, and my mother was busy with housekeeping. I was not taught anything and I was glad of it. No one ever gave me any lessons. Very early in the morning I used to run off to the pond, or to the woods, or to the haymaking, or to the harvesters—I did not mind the sun scorching me or getting lost far from our village, or getting scratched by scrambling through bushes, or tearing my dress—I got scolded at home later, but I did not care.

I can't help thinking that if I had not left the country and had lived in the same place all my life, I should always have been happy. And yet I had to leave the place where I was born while still a child. I was only twelve when we went to live in Petersburg. I still feel sad when I remember our mournful preparations to leave the country, how I wept when saying good-bye to everything that was dear to me. I remember flinging myself on my father's neck and imploring him, with tears in my eyes, to stay in the country a little longer. Father shouted at me; mother cried and said that we had to go, that business matters made it necessary. The old Prince P. had died. His heirs had dismissed my father from his post. Father had some money invested privately in Petersburg. In the hope of improving his circumstances, he thought his personal presence in Petersburg was necessary. I was told all this later by my mother. We settled down in a Petersburg suburb and lived in the same place until my father's death.

I found it so difficult to get used to my new life. We arrived in Petersburg in the autumn. The day we left the country was so bright, so warm, so full of sunshine; work in the fields was just coming to an end, huge stacks of corn were piled up on the threshing-floors and clamorous flocks of birds were flying over them; everything was so bright and gay, while here, on our arrival in the capital, we were met by rain, damp autumn hoar-frost, foul weather, slush, and crowds of new, unfamiliar faces, looking cross, inhospitable, discontented. We managed to settle down. I remember how busy we all were, how much time we spent rushing about, getting new household things. My father was hardly ever at home, my mother had few spare moments—I seem to have been completely forgotten. I felt so unhappy getting up in the morning after the first night in our new home. Our windows looked out onto some sort of a brownish fence. The street below was always filthy. There were few passers-by, and all of them were wrapped up tightly, all of them were so cold.

At home it was so dreadfully dull and dreary. We had hardly any relatives or friends. My father had quarrelled with Anna Fyodorovna (he seemed to owe her money). People came to see us quite often on business. They usually wrangled loudly and shouted. After such visits my father would look discontented and cross. He would pace the room for hours, knitting his brows and not uttering a word to anyone. My mother, not daring to address him at these moments, was silent. I would sit in some corner, reading a book —quietly, silently, not daring to stir.

Three months after our arrival in Petersburg I was sent to a boarding-school. You can't imagine how sad I felt at first among strange people. Everything was so cold and unfriendly: the mistresses always shouting at me, the girls always making fun of me, and me, so timid and shy! So strict, so exacting! Every hour allotted for something, eating together, boring teachers —all this worried and tortured me terribly at first. I could not sleep there. I used to cry all through the night—a long tedious, chilly night. In the evenings, everyone would be doing homework, while I sat over a vocabulary or tried to learn by heart some dialogue, not daring to stir, all the time thinking of home, of my father and mother, of my old nanny and the fairy-tales she used to tell me. . . . How terribly sad I felt! The most trifling thing at home—I'd remember even that with pleasure. I kept thinking and thinking—how lovely it would be at home now! I'd be sitting in our little room at tea with my parents. It would be so warm, so nice, so familiar! How warmly, how tightly, I'd have embraced my mother now! I'd be thinking and thinking of it and then start weeping quietly, choking back the tears, and I'd forget all about my homework. When I failed to do my work for the next day, I'd dream all night about my teachers, the headmistress and the girls. I'd keep repeating my lessons all night while asleep, but next day I wouldn't know a thing. They'd make me kneel as a punishment and give me only one meal that day. I felt so dull and cheerless. At first, all the girls used to laugh at me, tease me and put me off whenever I was learning my lessons. They used to pinch me on our way to dinner or tea, and complain about me for no reason to the class mistress. But, oh, the joy when my nanny used to come to fetch me on Saturday evenings! I'd embrace the dear old woman in a frenzy of delight. She'd dress me, wrap me up and scarcely be able to keep pace with me on the way home. I'd chatter and chatter and tell her all about the school. I'd arrive home merry and gay, embrace my parents as warmly as though I'd not seen them for ten years. We'd tell each other the latest news, we'd talk, we'd tell stories. I'd greet everyone, laugh, rock with laughter, run, skip. My father would start talking seriously to me about my lessons, my teachers, the French language and Lomond's grammar—yet we were all so happy and contented. I feel happy even now when I think of those moments. I did my best to learn my lessons to please my father. I could see that he was spending his last penny on me, while he, himself, was struggling to keep his head above water. Every day he grew more gloomy, more discontented, more cross-tempered; his character deteriorated completely; his business affairs were not prospering; his debts increased to an alarming extent. My mother was afraid to cry, afraid to utter a word for fear of angering my father. She fell ill, grew thinner and thinner, and began to cough painfully. Whenever I came home from school, I would find everybody looking sad. My mother would be crying quietly, my father would be in a bad temper. They'd start bickering and reproaching each other. Father would start saying that I was giving him no pleasure, that I was no comfort to him, that they had sacrificed everything for me and that I still could not speak French. In short, mother and I were blamed for all his failures, for all his misfortunes, for everything. Poor mother, how could he torture her so? It used to break my heart to see: her cheeks had grown hollow, her eyes were sunken, her face was covered by a consumptive flush. But it was I who caught it most of all. It would begin with some trifle and end with goodness only knows what. I would often myself not know what it was all about. The things I was held to be blamed for: that I knew no French, that I was a great fool, that the headmistress of my school was a negligent, stupid woman, that she cared nothing about our morals, that father had so far been unable to get a job, that Lomond's grammar was a rotten grammar, that Zapolsky's grammar was much better, that he had wasted a lot of money on me, that I had no feelings, that I was heartless—in short, however much I tried to learn French words and conversation pieces, I was to blame for everything, I had to answer for everything. It was not that my father did not love me: he simply doted on me and mother. But he was like that—his character was like that.

Cares, worries, disappointments and failures exhausted my poor father to such an extent that he became distrustful and acrimonious. He was frequently near despair; he began to neglect his health; and suddenly, after a short, painful illness, he died so unexpectedly that for some days we were beside ourselves with shock. My mother was in such a state of torpor

that I was afraid for her reason. The moment my father was dead, his creditors appeared as though out of the blue. Crowds of them filled our house. We gave away all we possessed. Our little suburban house, which my father had bought six months after our arrival in Petersburg, had also to be sold. I don't know how things were settled in the end, but we found ourselves without a roof over our heads and without a penny. My mother was suffering from a wasting malady, we had nothing to live on, and ruin was staring us in the face. I was only fourteen. It was then that Anna Fyodorovna came to see us. She kept saying that she was a gentlewoman and a relative of ours. My mother, too, said she was a relative, but a very distant one. She never came to see us while my father was alive. Now she appeared with tears in her eyes, and after declaring that she was greatly concerned about us and condoling with us on our bereavement and our desperate situation, she said that it was all my father's fault because he had lived beyond his means, had been over-ambitious, and had relied too much on himself. She expressed a wish to become closer friends with us, proposed to forget our mutual disagreements, and when my mother declared that she had never harboured any ill-will against her, she burst into tears, took my mother to church and ordered mass to be said for the darling (as she described my father). After that she declared solemnly that she was now reconciled with my mother.

After a great deal of talking and cautionary preambles in which she described our desperate situation, our destitution, hopelessness and helplessness in vivid colours, she invited us, as she herself expressed it, to take refuge at her house. My mother thanked her but could not make up her mind for a long time. But as there was nothing else to be done and as there was no other way out of our difficulties, she at last told Anna Fyodorovna that we accepted her offer with gratitude. I can still remember the morning when we moved from our suburb to Vassilevsky Island. It was a clear, dry, frosty autumn morning. My mother cried, and I, too, felt terribly depressed. My heart seemed to be breaking with inexpressible, terrible anguish. . . . It was a hard time.

2.

At first, I mean before mother and myself grew used to our new surroundings, we found living with Anna Fyodorovna strange and frightening. Anna Fyodorovna lived in her own house in Sixth Street. The house consisted of five clean rooms, three of which were occupied by Anna Fyodorovna and my cousin, Sasha, an orphan child, whom Anna Fyodorovna had brought up. Mother and myself lived in one room and in the next room to ours lived a lodger, a poor student by the name of Pokrovsky. Anna Fyodorovna lived very well, much better than could have been expected; but her financial position was a bit of a mystery, as were her occupations. She was always in a rush, always worried, left the house on foot or in a cab several times a day, but what she did, what she was worried about and to what purpose, I could not find out. She had a wide and varied circle of friends. Lots of people continuously called on her, but goodness only knows who they were or what their business was. They never stayed long. My mother always took me to our room

as soon as the doorbell rang. This made Anna Fyodorovna very angry with my mother, and she kept saying
that we were much too proud, considering our station
in life. She went on talking for hours like that. At the
time I could not understand these accusations of
pride, for it is only now that I have realised, or at least
guessed, why my mother was so much against living
with Anna Fyodorovna. Anna was a bad, wicked
woman. She made life unbearable for us. It is still a
mystery to me why she asked us to go and live with
her. At first she was quite nice to us, but afterwards,
when she saw how helpless we were and that we had
nowhere to go, she showed herself in her true colours.
Later on she became very affectionate towards me,
even coarsely affectionate, somehow, even going so
far as to flatter me, but at first I, too, suffered together
with my mother. She kept constantly reproaching us
and reminding us every moment of her benefactions.
She used to introduce us to strangers as her poor rela-
tions, as a helpless widow and an orphan girl whom
she had given shelter, acts of kindness, and Christian
love. She watched every mouthful we took at table,
and if we did not eat, the same old business started
again: so we were too proud, were we? She was very
sorry she could not afford to entertain us any better
and indeed she doubted whether we were used to anything better. She never stopped reviling my father
who, she said, had wished to be better than other people, but had made an awful mess of things: he had
left his wife and daughter penniless, and if we had not
found a charitable, compassionate Christian soul, we
might, for all she knew, have died of hunger in the
street. What didn't she say? To hear her was not so

much distressing as disgusting. My mother never stopped crying, her health grew worse from day to day, she was visibly wasting away, and yet she and I went on working from morning until night. We had received dressmaking orders, which did not please Anna Fyodorovna at all. She kept telling us that her house was not a dressmaking establishment. But we had to get clothes to wear and to save up some money for unforeseen expenses; in short, we had to have money of our own. Anyway, we kept saving up in the hope of one day being able to move elsewhere. But my mother could not bear the strain of work and she grew weaker every day. Illness, like a canker, was visibly gnawing at her life, drawing her nearer and nearer to the grave. I saw it all, I felt it all, I endured it all: it all took place before my eyes!

Days passed, and every day was like the last one. We lived quietly, just as if we were not living in town at all. Little by little Anna Fyodorovna calmed down, having realised at last her power over us. Not that anyone thought of contradicting her. Our room was divided from her part of the house by a corridor, and, as I have already mentioned, next to us lived Pokrovsky. He taught Sasha French, German, history and geography—all the sciences, as Anna Fyodorovna used to say, and in return received free board and lodgings. Sasha was a very intelligent girl, though high-spirited and wilful. She was thirteen at that time. Anna Fyodorovna remarked to my mother that it would not be a bad thing if I, too, took some lessons, seeing that I had not finished school. My mother gratefully agreed, and I joined Sasha for a year taking lessons from Pokrovsky.

Pokrovsky was a poor, a very poor young man; because of his ill health he was not able to take a regular university course, but we still called him a student. He lived so quietly, inoffensively and self-effacingly that we never even heard him reading aloud in his room. He looked rather peculiar too: he walked so awkwardly, he bowed so clumsily, he spoke so strangely that at first I could not look at him without laughing. Sasha was always playing tricks on him, especially during our lessons. He was, besides, easily exasperated; he was always cross, flew into a rage over the least trifle, shouted at us, complained of our conduct, and often retired angrily to his room before the end of our lessons. In his room he would sit for days over his books. He had a good many books, all of them very rare and expensive. He seemed to have other lessons, too, was paid a salary, and the moment he had a little money, spent it on books.

In time I got to know him better and more intimately. He was a very kind and worthy man, one of the best one could happen to meet. My mother respected him greatly. Later, he became one of my best friends, too—after my mother, of course.

Grown girl though I was, I joined Sasha, at first, in playing pranks on our teacher. We would spend hours trying to think of something that would exasperate him and make him lose his patience. He was very funny when he was angry, and it used to amuse us very much. (I am ashamed to recall it now.) Once when we had reduced him nearly to tears, I heard him whisper: "Wicked children!" I felt embarrassed, I was both ashamed and sick at heart and sorry for him. I remember turning red in the face and I began begging him,

almost in tears, to calm down and not to take any notice of our stupid pranks. But he closed the book and
went back to his room. All that day I was torn with
remorse. The thought that we children had driven
him to tears by our cruel behaviour was unendur-
able. We must have expected him to burst into tears.
We must have wanted it. We had succeeded in ex-
asperating him, which meant that we forced him, the
poor, unhappy man, to remember his cruel lot. I could
not sleep all night with vexation, grief, and remorse.
People say that remorse relieves one's feelings, but the
contrary is true. I don't see how my grief could awaken
my feeling of self-respect. I did not want him to think
that I was a child. I was fifteen then. From that day I
became obsessed with the idea of finding ways of making Pokrovsky change his opinion of me. I made thou-
sands of plans, but I was often timid and shy and in
my present position I could not make up my mind and
indulged in all sorts of dreams (and goodness knows
what dreams!). But I no longer joined Sasha in playing
the fool, and he was no longer angry with us. But that
was not enough to satisfy my self-esteem.

Now I must say a few words about the strangest,
the most curious, and the most pitiable man I have
ever happened to come across. I speak of him now, at
this particular point in my journal, because until that
very moment I had hardly paid any attention to him—
to such an extent had everything that concerned Pokrovsky suddenly become of absorbing interest to me.

A little, grey-haired old man used to visit our house
sometimes. He was dirty, badly dressed, awkward, un-
gainly—in short, as strange-looking as could be. At
first glance one got the impression that he was

ashamed of himself for some reason. That was why he was so ill-at-ease, why he had such awkward gestures. Indeed, he had such strange mannerisms that one could not help concluding that he was not in his right mind. He used to arrive at our house and remain standing in the hall by the glass doors, not daring to enter. If anyone—Sasha, a maid or myself—happened to pass whom he knew to be well-disposed towards him, he would begin to wave and beckon and make all sorts of signs, and it was only when that person nodded or called him in—the agreed sign that there was no visitor in the house and that he could come in when he liked—it was only then that the old man opened the door quietly, smiled happily, rubbed his hands with satisfaction, and tiptoed into Pokrovsky's room. The old man was Pokrovsky's father.

Later I came to know the story of that poor old man. He had a job in some government office but, possessing no abilities of any kind, had occupied a very low, insignificant post in the civil service. After his first wife (Pokrovsky's mother) had died, he took it into his head to marry again, this time a shopkeeper's daughter. His second wife turned the whole house upside down, made life a hell for everybody, and took everybody in hand. Pokrovsky junior was still a child at the time, about ten years old. His stepmother hated him. But Fate favoured the little boy. A landowner by the name of Bykov, who had known Pokrovsky senior and had formerly helped him financially, took the boy under his wing and placed him in a prep school. He took an interest in the boy because he had known his mother, on whom Anna Fyodorovna had heaped benefits and married off to Pokrovsky. Mr. Bykov, a close friend of Anna Fyodorovna's, in a fit of magnanimity, had given the bride a dowry of five thousand roubles. Where the money had gone remains a mystery. It was Anna Fyodorovna herself who told me about it, for the student Pokrovsky never liked to discuss his family affairs. His mother was said to have been very beautiful, and I couldn't help wondering why she should have married so insignificant a man. . . . She died young—four years after her wedding.

From the prep school Pokrovsky went to a grammar school and from there to the university. Mr. Bykov, who very frequently visited Petersburg, continued to patronise the young man, who was unable to continue his university studies because of ill health. It was then that Mr. Bykov introduced him to Anna Fyodorovna and personally recommended him to her. It was in this way that young Pokrovsky obtained board and lodgings on condition that he teach Sasha all that was required.

Old man Pokrovsky, driven to desperation by his wife's cruelties, gave himself up to a life of dissipation and was hardly ever sober. His wife beat him and made him live in the kitchen. She brought him to such a state that in the end he got used to blows and ill treatment and no longer complained. He was not yet really old, but his bad habits had almost driven him out of his mind. The only sign of decent human feelings was his great love for his son, who was said to bear a striking resemblance to his mother. Was it the memory of his first kind wife that was responsible for his great love for his son? The old man would not speak of anything else but his son and he visited the boy twice a week without fail. He dared not come more

often because young Pokrovsky hated his father's
visits. The chief and most important of his faults was
his lack of respect for his father. No doubt his father
sometimes was the most obnoxious man in the world.
To begin with, he was terribly inquisitive and, besides,
by his conversation and his most insipid and inane
questions, he constantly interfered with his son's studies, not to mention the fact that he sometimes arrived
drunk. Gradually, however, the son weaned his father
from his evil ways, from inquisitiveness and everlasting chatter, and in the end got the old man to listen
to him as though he were an oracle, and the father
dared not open his mouth without his son's permis-
sion. The poor old fellow could not help admiring and
doting on Petenka (as he called his son, Peter). Yet,
when he came to see him, the old man almost always
looked tired and worried, probably because he was
uncertain about the reception he might expect from
his son. As a rule, he could not bring himself to enter
the room for a long time, and when I happened to be
there, he would question me for about twenty minutes
as to whether his Petenka was well, what sort of mood
he was in, whether he was engaged on some important
work, what exactly he was doing, whether he was writing something, or whether he was lost in meditation.
When I had sufficiently encouraged and reassured the
old man, he would at last make up his mind to go in.
He would open the door very quietly and very cautiously, first poke his head through the door, and if he
saw that his son was not cross and nodded to him to
come in, he would enter the room, take off his ragged
overcoat and his hat, which was crumpled and in holes
and with a torn brim, hang them up on a hook—

quietly and without a sound. Next he would carefully sit down somewhere on a chair and, without taking his eyes off his son, follow his every movement in an effort to discover his Petenka's mood. If his son did not appear to be in a very good mood, the old fellow would notice it, would get up from his seat at once, and after remarking, "I've only looked in for a moment, Petenka," go on to explain that he had been out "for a long walk" and happened "to pass by" and dropped in "for a rest." He then would silently and humbly put on his coat and hat and, opening the door quietly again, go out, forcing himself to smile so as to conceal his aching heart from his son.

But when the son was glad to see his father, the old man would be struck dumb with joy. His face beamed with pleasure, and this could be detected in his gestures and movements. If his son spoke to him, the old man would invariably rise a little in his chair and reply quietly, humbly, almost reverentially, always trying to choose the choicest, that is to say, the most ridiculous, expressions. But the gift of words did not come easy to him: he would always grow confused, he would lose courage, so that he would not know what to do with his hands or with himself, and a long time afterwards he would whisper his answer, as though wishing to correct himself. If, however, he succeeded in giving a good answer, he would sit up happily, straighten his waistcoat, cravat and frockcoat, and assume an air of self-conscious dignity. Occasionally, indeed, he would feel so emboldened, he would let his courage go so far as to get up quietly from his chair, walk up to the bookshelves, take out a book and even proceed to read something, whatever the book hap-

pened to be. All this he would do with an air of
feigned indifference and self-composure, as though he
could always do as he liked with his son's books, as
though his son's kindness was nothing unusual as far
as he was concerned. Yet one day I chanced to see the
poor old man frightened when his son told him not to
touch his books. He grew confused, hastened to put
the book back, but did so upside down, then, wishing
to put it right, turned it with its back to the wall,
smiled, blushed, and was at a loss as to how to make
amends for his misdemeanour. Pokrovsky, by his
hints, gradually weaned his father from his bad habits,
and whenever his father was sober three times running, he gave him a quarter or half a rouble or even
more on parting. Sometimes he would buy his father a
pair of boots or a tie or a waistcoat. The old fellow
would be as proud of his new acquisition as a peacock.
Sometimes he would pay us a visit. He would bring
Sasha and me gingerbread birds or apples and keep
talking to us about his Petenka. He would ask us to do
our lessons well and do as his son told us. Petenka, he
used to say, was a good son, an exemplary son, and,
last but not least, a learned son. While saying that, he
would wink at us with his left eye so funnily and pull
such funny faces that we could not refrain from laughing, and we laughed heartily. My mother was very fond
of him. But the old man detested Anna Fyodorovna,
though in her presence he was as meek as a lamb.

Soon I stopped taking lessons from Pokrovsky. He
still regarded me as a child, a frivolous young girl, just
as he did Sasha. This hurt me very much because I
did my best to make up for my former behaviour. But
no one took any notice of me. This exasperated me

more and more. I hardly ever spoke to Pokrovsky out of school hours and, indeed, could not bring myself to do so. I used to blush, grow confused, and then cry with vexation in a corner.

I don't know how it would have ended had not a strange circumstance helped to break the ice between us. One evening, when mother was sitting in Anna Fyodorovna's room, I stole into Pokrovsky's room. I knew that he was out and honestly don't know what made me go there. Before that I never so much as looked into his room although we had lived next door to him for over a year. This time my heart pounded violently, so violently that it seemed almost on the point of leaping out of my breast. I looked round with a special kind of curiosity. Pokrovsky's room was very poorly furnished; there was no attempt to keep things in order. Five long bookshelves with books were fixed to the walls. Papers lay on the table and chairs. Books and papers! A strange thought struck me, and at the same time I was overcome by an unpleasant feeling of vexation. It seemed to me that my friendship, my loving heart meant little to him. He was an educated man, while I was a silly creature who knew nothing and had never read a single book. I looked enviously at the long bookshelves which were crammed with books. I was seized by a feeling of vexation, anguish, and a kind of frenzy. I felt that I had to read those books and I made up my mind to read them, one by one, as soon as possible. I don't know but perhaps I thought that by learning everything he knew, I should be more worthy of his friendship. I rushed towards the shelves and, without stopping to think, seized hold of the first dirty old volume. Blushing and going pale in turn, trembling with fear and excitement, I took the stolen book back to my room with the intention of reading it through at night, after my mother had fallen asleep, by the light of the night candle.

But you can imagine my annoyance when, after returning to our room, I discovered that it was an old, battered, and worm-eaten Latin book. Without a moment's hesitation, I went back to Pokrovsky's room. I was just about to replace the book on the shelf when I became aware of a noise in the corridor and someone's approaching footsteps. There was no time to lose. I quickly tried to replace the tiresome book, but it had been wedged so tightly that after I had taken it out the other books had closed up and left no space for their former comrade. I had not the strength to insert the book. Instead, I gave a mighty pull at the books on the shelf. The rusty nail on which the shelf rested (and which seemed to be waiting on purpose for the right time to break off) snapped off. One end of the shelf crashed down, scattering the books on the floor. At that moment the door opened, and Pokrovsky walked into the room.

I must point out here that Pokrovsky could not bear anyone interfering with the things in his room. Ill betide the person who as much as touched his books! You can, therefore, imagine my horror when books—big and small, of every shape and size and thickness—precipitated themselves from the shelf and came flying and jumping about under the table and the chairs and all over the room. I'd have liked to run, but it was too late. "Of course," I thought to myself, "it's all over. I am lost, ruined! I'm misbehaving, playing about like a ten-year-old child! I'm a stupid, mischievous girl! I'm a great fool!" Pokrovsky was very angry. "Well, I must say!" he shouted, "that's the limit! Aren't you ashamed to go on like this? Won't you ever stop fooling around?" And he rushed to pick up the books. I bent down to help him. "Don't bother! Don't bother!" he shouted. "You'd have done better not to have come where you're not wanted!" But a little mollified by my contrite look, he went on more quietly to admonish me, taking advantage of his former rights as a teacher. "Tell me, when will you take hold of yourself and change your ways? Just look at you! You're no longer a child, a little girl. You're fifteen already!" And, no doubt, wishing to make sure I really was no longer a little girl, he looked at me and blushed to the roots of his hair. I could not understand why he blushed; I stood gazing at him in astonishment. He got up from the floor, came up to me, looking embarrassed and covered with confusion, murmured something, seemed to apologise for something, perhaps for not having noticed that I was now a grown-up girl. At last I understood. I don't know what I was feeling at that moment; I, too, grew terribly confused. I did not know what to do and blushed even more than Pokrovsky. Covering my face with my hands, I rushed out of the room.

I did not know what to do or where to hide myself for shame. The fact alone that he had found me in his room was bad enough! For three whole days I dared not look at him. I blushed so violently that tears came to my eyes. My head was full of all sorts of strange and ridiculous thoughts. One of them—the craziest—was that I should go to Pokrovsky, tell him frankly, confess everything, everything, and assure him that I had not acted like a silly girl, but with good intention. Indeed, I almost made up my mind to go, but thank goodness, had not enough courage to do so! I can just imagine the mess I'd have made of it! Even now I'm ashamed to think of it.

A few days later, my mother suddenly fell dangerously ill. For two days she did not leave her bed and on the third night she ran a high temperature and was delirious. I did not sleep all night, looking after my mother, sitting by her bed, giving her water to drink, and seeing that she had her medicine at the appointed hours. The next night I felt utterly exhausted. Every now and then I dozed off, everything went swimming before my eyes, I felt dizzy and was about to faint any moment from sheer exhaustion. But the weak moans of my mother aroused me. I gave a start, awoke for a moment, only to be once again overcome by drowsiness. I felt dreadful. I don't know —I can't remember—but a kind of awful dream, a kind of terrible vision visited my overwrought brain during the agonising moment of the struggle between sleep and wakefulness. I awoke in terror. It was dark in the room, the night-light was about to go out, shifts of light suddenly lit up the whole room, flickered for a moment or two on the walls, and then disappeared completely. I was panic-stricken for some reason, I was seized by a kind of horror—my imagination had been overexcited by my terrible dream, my heart was contracted with anguish. . . . I leaped from the chair and, unable to control myself, uttered a scream, wrung from me by some terrible, agonising, distressful feeling. At that moment the door opened and Pokrovsky entered the room.

All I can remember is that I came to in his arms. He carefully put me down in an armchair, handed me a glass of water, and overwhelmed me with questions. I don't remember what I told him in reply. "You're ill," he said, touching my hand, "you're very ill. You have a high temperature, you're destroying yourself, you're neglecting your own health. Compose yourself, lie down, go to sleep. I'll waken you in two hours, get some rest. . . . Lie down, lie down!" He went on, without letting me say a word in protest. Fatigue had robbed me of all my strength, my eyes were closing from weariness. I lay down in the armchair, thinking of going to sleep for half an hour, but I slept until morning. Pokrovsky wakened me only when it was time to give my mother her medicine.

When, the next evening at about eleven o'clock, after I had had a little rest during the day, I was getting ready once more to spend the night in an armchair at my mother's bedside (having made up my mind firmly not to fall asleep this time), Pokrovsky knocked at the door. I opened it. "I expect you must find it dull to sit by yourself," he said, "so I brought you a book. Take it, please. It will help you to while away the time." I took the book. I don't remember what book it was: I don't think I even opened it, though I did not sleep all night. A great feeling of excitement was preventing me from sleeping. I could not stay in one place. I got up from my chair several times and began pacing the room. I was overwhelmed by a powerful feeling of contentment. I was so glad of Pokrovsky's attention. I was proud that he should be so anxious and worried about me. I spent the whole night thinking and dreaming about it. Pokrovsky did not come in again, and I knew he would not come and wondered whether he would come the following evening.

That evening, when everyone in the house had gone to bed, Pokrovsky opened his door and began a conversation with me from the threshold of his room. I can't remember a single word of what we said to each other that night. All I remember is that I blushed, felt embarrassed, was vexed with myself, and waited with impatience for the end of the conversation, though I myself had wanted it to take place, though I had been dreaming of it all day and inventing all sorts of questions and replies. That evening saw the beginning of our friendship, and all through my mother's illness we spent several hours together each night. Gradually I overcame my shyness, though after each of these conversations there was still something I felt vexed about with myself. However, I could not help observing with secret joy and a proud feeling of pleasure that I made him forget his tiresome books. By sheer chance, as a jest, our conversation turned upon their falling from the shelf. It was a rather peculiar moment. I seemed somehow to be a little too frank and open-hearted. I was carried away by a feeling of excitement and strange elation and I made a clean breast of everything—that I longed to study, that I was eager to know something, that I resented being taken for a little girl, a child. I expect that I was in a very strange frame of mind: my heart was melting with tenderness, there were tears in my eyes —and I did not conceal anything from him. I told him everything, everything, about my feeling of friendship for him, my desire to love him, to live with him in love and friendship, to comfort him, to put his mind at rest. He gave me a strange look. He was embarrassed, astonished, but said nothing. I felt suddenly terribly hurt and sad. I thought he did not understand me, that he was, perhaps, laughing at me. I suddenly burst into tears, sobbing like a child. I could not restrain myself, just as though I were having some hysterical fit. He seized my hands, kissed them, clasped them to his breast; he implored me to compose myself; he tried to comfort me. He was deeply touched. I can't remember what he said to me, but I cried, laughed, cried again, blushed, and could not utter a word for joy. Yet in spite of my agitation, I noticed that there still remained a kind of air of embarrassment and constraint about Pokrovsky. It seemed to me that he could not help feeling greatly surprised at my raptures, my enthusiasm—at such sudden ardent and passionate friendship. Perhaps he was just interested at first; afterwards his hesitation vanished and he accepted my devotion, my words of friendship and my concern with the same simple and frank feelings that I had experienced, and responded to them with the same concern and friendliness and devotion just as a sincere friend and a brother would do. Oh, my heart felt so warm, so happy! I had concealed nothing, repressed nothing. He saw it all and each day became more and more attached to me.

I do not honestly remember what we talked about during those painful and yet rapturous hours of our meetings each night by the flickering light of the icon-lamp and almost at the very bedside of my poor, sick mother! We talked about everything that came into our heads, that escaped from our hearts, that asked to be said—and we were almost happy. . . . Oh, dear, it was a sad and happy time—everything together, and I am both happy and sad when I think of it now. Memories, whether happy or bitter, are always painful; at least, that's how I feel about them, but the pain, too, is sweet. When one feels depressed, hurt, jaded or sad, memories revive and freshen one, as dewdrops on a humid evening after a hot day refresh and revive a poor, wilted flower burnt by the scorching heat of the day.

My mother was recovering, but I still continued to sit by her bedside at night. Pokrovsky often gave me books. At first, I used to read them to keep awake, then I read more carefully and at last with avidity; I suddenly became aware of a great deal that was new, unknown, and unfamiliar to me. New ideas, new impressions all at once rushed like a violent torrent into my mind. And the more emotion, the more confusion and labour it cost me to absorb these new impressions, the dearer they were to me, the more delightfully did they stir me to the very depths of my soul. They crowded into my mind all at once, all of a sudden, giving it no time to rest. My whole being was troubled by a kind of strange chaos. But this spiritual ferment was unable, was not strange enough, to throw me into utter confusion. I was too much of a dreamer, and that saved me.

When my mother recovered from her illness, our nocturnal meetings and long conversations came to an end. Occasionally we managed to exchange a few words with each other, often meaningless and of little importance, though I liked to attach some significance to everything, to give everything its special, imaginary value. My life was full, I was happy, quietly, peacefully happy. Several weeks passed like that.

One day Pokrovsky senior came to see us. He chatted a long time with us; he was extraordinarily cheerful, genial, garrulous. He laughed, cracked his usual jokes, and, at last, solved the riddle of his enthusiasm by telling us that in exactly one week's time it would be his Petenka's birthday and that in honour of the occasion he meant to pay a visit to his son wearing a new waistcoat and a new pair of shoes which his wife had promised to buy him. In short, the old man was as happy as a sandboy and chatted about everything that happened to enter his head.

His birthday! That birthday gave me no rest by day or night. I resolved to remind Pokrovsky of my friendship by giving him a present. But what kind of present? At last I decided to give him books. I knew that he wanted to have a complete set of Pushkin's works in its last edition, and I decided to buy Pushkin. I had my own thirty roubles which I had earned by my needlework. I had saved that money to buy myself a dress. I sent our cook, old Matryona, to find out the price of such a complete set of Pushkin's works. Alas, the price of the eleven volumes, including the extra price for the binding, would amount to at least sixty roubles. Where was I to get the money? I thought and thought, but did not know what to do. I was loath to ask mother. She would most certainly have helped me, but in that case everyone in the house would have learned about my present, and the present itself would have been in the nature of a recompense, of a payment for the trouble Pokrovsky had taken on my behalf during the past year. What I wanted was to give him a present from myself, without anybody's knowledge. As for the trouble he had taken I should have liked to be beholden to him forever without any payment except my friendship. At last I thought of a way out of the difficulty.

I knew that at the bookstalls in the Arcade one could sometimes buy a second-hand or even almost-new book at half its price, provided one haggled over it. I, therefore, decided to go to the Arcade at the first opportunity. This occurred the very next day. As my mother was not feeling well and Anna Fyodorovna, fortunately, was too busy to go out, I did the shopping and left for the Arcade together with Matryona. Luckily, I soon found a set of Pushkin's works, rather handsomely bound. I began to bargain for it. At first I was asked more for it than I would have been asked in a shop, but afterwards, not without difficulty, for I had to pretend to go away a few times, I forced the stall-holder to lower his price to ten roubles in silver. I did enjoy the bargaining! Poor Matryona did not know what had become of me and why I wanted to buy so many books. But imagine my horror when I found that I had only thirty roubles in notes and the stall-holder refused to reduce the price still more. In the end, after I had entreated him again and again, he relented, but reduced the price only by two and a half roubles. He swore that he made that reduction only for my sake, because I was such a nice young lady, and that he would not have done it for anyone else. But I was still short of two and a half roubles! I was ready to burst into tears, but a most unforeseen circumstance came to my rescue.

Not far away, at another bookstall, I saw Pokrovsky senior, surrounded by four or five booksellers and
looking utterly bewildered and confused. Each of
them was offering him all sorts of books, and he would
have liked to buy any of them. The poor old man
looked frightened and stupefied and unable to make
up his mind what to buy. I went up to him and asked
what he was doing there. The old man was very glad
to see me, for he was very fond of me, almost no less
than of his Petenka. "Why, I am buying some books,
my dear young lady," he replied. "I'm buying books
for my Peter. It will be his birthday soon and he loves
books, so I am buying some books for him."

The old man always spoke rather comically and now
he was, besides, in a terrible state of confusion. Whatever he tried to buy cost either a rouble in silver, or
two or three roubles in silver. He stopped bidding for
large books, but merely gazed enviously at them, fin-
gered their pages, turned them over and over in his
hands, and then replaced them. "No, no," he murmured to himself, "that is too dear. Let's try something
else from this lot. . . ." And he started fingering
thin, paper-bound volumes, collections of folksongs,
almanacs—they were all much cheaper. "But why are
you buying all those?" I asked him. "They're such terrible rubbish." "Why, not at all," he replied. "Just have
a look at the good books they have here. Yes, indeed,
very good books!" The last words he uttered in so
plaintive a sing-song that I could not help feeling that
he was ready to burst into tears from vexation that
good books were so dear, and that any moment a tear
would drop from his pale cheeks onto his red nose. I
asked him how much money he had. "Why," the poor

old fellow replied, taking out his money wrapped in a piece of dirty newspaper and counting it, "fifty copecks in copper." I dragged him off at once to my stallholder. "Here are eleven volumes which cost only thirty-two and a half roubles. I have thirty, add those two and a half roubles and we'll buy the books together and make them a joint present." The old man was overjoyed, emptied all his money onto the stall, and the stallholder loaded him with the library we now owned in common. The dear old man stuffed the books in all his pockets, carried them in and under his arms and took them away to his place, promising to bring them all back secretly to me the next day.

Next day the old man came to see his son, spent an hour with him as usual, and afterwards came to see us. He sat down beside me with a most comical and mysterious expression on his face. Smiling and rubbing his hands with pleasure and pride at being in possession of a secret, he informed me that he had stealthily transferred the books to our apartment and placed them in a corner of the kitchen under Matryona's protection. Then the conversation quite naturally passed to the coming celebration. The old man was expatiating on the way we would offer our present, and the more he became absorbed in the subject, the more he talked, the more obvious it became to me that he had something on his mind that he could not, dared not, indeed was afraid to divulge. I waited and kept silent. The hidden joy, the hidden pleasure that I detected so easily in his strange antics, his grimaces and left-eye winks had disappeared. He grew more troubled and looked more wistful. At last he could restrain himself no longer. "Listen," he began timidly in an undertone. "Listen, my dear Barbara . . . do you know what?" The old man looked terribly embarrassed. "You see, on his birthday, I think you should take *ten* books and give them to him yourself, I mean, as your present, and I will take only one—the eleventh book—and give it to him as my present, I mean, as my own contribution. So, you see, you will have something for him and I, too, will have something to give him." At that point the old man got utterly confused and fell silent. I looked at him: he was waiting for my verdict with timid anticipation. "But don't you want us to give our present together, Mr. Pokrovsky?" I asked. "Well, you see, it's—er—you see, it's not quite —er—" In short, the old man looked embarrassed, blushed, got stuck in his sentence, and could not carry on.

"You see," he explained, at last, "I indulge myself sometimes. . . . I mean to say, I almost always indulge myself, always . . . doing something I know to be bad. . . . I mean, sometimes it's so terribly cold, and sometimes there are all sorts of such aggravating things, or you just feel depressed, or something unpleasant happens, and—er—I can't control myself, I mean, I sometimes drink too much. Peter doesn't like it, you know. He gets angry, you see, and he scolds me and lectures me about it. So, you see, I'd like to show him by my present that I'm going to turn over a new leaf and begin to behave decently, that I saved up to buy him a book, have been saving up for a long time because I hardly ever have any money except when Peter happens to give me some. He knows that. Therefore, when he sees what use I have made of his money, he will realise that I have done it for his sake alone."

I felt terribly sorry for the old man. I didn't hesitate very long. The old man looked anxiously at me. "Look here, Mr. Pokrovsky," I said, "you give him all the books." "All the books? What do you mean?" "Yes, all the books." "From me?" "From you." "From me alone? I mean, as my own present?" "Yes, as your own present." I seemed to have spoken clearly enough, but the old man did not seem to grasp my meaning for a long time.

"Well, of course," he said, "that would be excellent, that would be splendid, but what about you?"

"Well, I won't give him anything."

"What!" the old man exclaimed almost in dismay, "You won't give anything to my darling son. Don't you want to give him anything?"

The old man looked startled. At that moment he was ready to give up his own suggestion so that I could give his son something. What a good soul! I assured the old man that I'd have been glad to give his son some present, but that I did not want to deprive the father of that pleasure. "If your son is pleased, and you are pleased," I said, "I shall be pleased also, for deep down in my heart I shall feel as though I had given him a present."

That completely reassured the old man. He spent another couple of hours at our place, though he could not sit still for a moment, getting up, playing about, talking boisterously, romping with Sasha, kissing us stealthily, pinching my arm, and secretly pulling faces at Anna Fyodorovna. In the end Anna Fyodorovna turned him out of the house. In short, the old man let himself go as he had, perhaps, never done before.

On the great day he arrived at exactly eleven
o'clock, straight from church, wearing his frock-coat,
which had been decently mended, and actually a new
waistcoat and a new pair of boots. He carried a pile of
books in his hands. We were sitting in Anna Fyodorovna's drawing-room at the time, having our coffee
(it was a Sunday). The old man began, I believe, by
saying that Pushkin was an extremely good poet,
then, getting rather confused and muddled, he suddenly went on to say that a man ought to behave properly instead of merely indulging himself and that bad
habits led to a man's ruin and destruction. He then
cited a few terrible examples of the evil consequences
of incontinence and concluded by saying that for some
time past he had completely reformed and that he was
behaving now in a most exemplary fashion. He had
(he added) felt the justice of his son's precepts before, indeed for a long time, and had locked it away
in his heart, but now he was, in fact, reforming in
good earnest and, to prove it, he was giving his son a
present of books he had bought on the money he had
been saving for a long time.

I could not refrain from laughing and crying as I
listened to the poor old fellow who certainly seemed
to be good at lying when the occasion required it. The
books were then transferred to Pokrovsky's room and
placed on a shelf. Pokrovsky at once guessed the
truth about them. The old man was invited to dinner.
That day we were all so happy. After dinner we
played at forfeits and cards. Sasha was in high spirits,
and I did not lag behind. Pokrovsky was very attentive to me and kept looking for an opportunity to talk

to me in private, but I would not let him. It was the happiest day I had known for four years.

But memories that follow are sad and painful. Now begins the story of my sombre days. That is why, perhaps, my pen begins to move more slowly, as though it were refusing to write any more. That is why, perhaps, I have gone over in my mind with such enthusiasm and such love the smallest details of my young life during those happy days. Those days did not last long; they were succeeded by sorrow, deep sorrow which will come to an end God only knows when.

My misfortunes began with the illness and death of Pokrovsky. He was taken ill two months after the events I have just described. During those two months he tried hard to obtain a livelihood, for until then he had had no secure job. Like all consumptives, he never —not up to the last moment—gave up hope of a long life. He had been offered a job as teacher in some town, but he had a great aversion to teaching. He could get no job in the civil service because of his poor health. Besides, he would have had to wait a long time for the first payment of his salary. In short, Pokrovsky could only anticipate failure everywhere. His character deteriorated, and his state of health worsened. He was not, however, aware of it. Autumn came. He went out every day, wearing only his light coat, in search of a job, feeling inwardly depressed. He got his feet wet, he got drenched in the rain and, finally, took to his bed and never got up again. . . . He died in the late autumn, at the end of October.

I hardly ever left his room throughout his illness, waiting on him and nursing him. Often I did not sleep for nights on end. He was rarely conscious and often delirious, when he would talk of goodness only knows what: of his job, of his books, of myself, of his father. It was then that I learned much about his circumstances I did not know and even had no idea of before. During the first days of his illness everyone in the house regarded me rather strangely, Anna Fyodorovna shaking her head deprecatingly. But I looked them all straight in the face, and they no longer blamed me for my concern for Pokrovsky—not my mother, at any rate.

Sometimes Pokrovsky knew who I was, but not often. He was unconscious almost the whole time. Sometimes he would talk to someone at night for a long, long time, uttering obscure, mysterious words, and in his narrow room, his hoarse voice re-echoed hollowly, as though in a tomb. I felt terrified at such times. During his last night, in particular, he acted like one in a frenzy; he suffered terribly, he was in agony; his moans wrung my heart. Everyone in the house seemed to be in a kind of state of terror. Anna Fyodorovna kept praying that God might take him as soon as possible. A doctor was summoned. The doctor said that the patient would quite certainly die in the morning.

Pokrovsky senior spent the whole of that night in the corridor, at the door of his son's room. They had put a straw mat for him there. He kept coming into the room every minute: he looked awful. He was so stricken with grief that he seemed to be completely bereft of feeling and sense. His head shook with fear. He trembled all over and kept muttering as though debating something with himself. I thought he'd go mad with grief.

Before dawn the old man, exhausted wi
agony, fell sound asleep on his straw mat.
o'clock, when his son was about to die, I
him. Pokrovsky had gained consciousness and bid farewell to us all. Funny! I could not cry, though my heart
was breaking. His last moments shattered and exhausted me completely. For a long, long time he
seemed to be asking for something with his failing
tongue, but I couldn't make any sense of his words.
My heart was bursting with pain. For a whole hour
he was tossing about, worrying about something, striv-
ing to make some sign with his hands that had grown
cold and numb. Then he again began asking me for
something plaintively in his hoarse, hollow voice; but
his words were just inarticulate sounds, and once more
I could make no sense of them. I brought everyone
in the house to his bedside, I gave him some water to
drink, but he just shook his head mournfully. At last
I understood what it was he wanted. He was asking me
to draw aside the curtains and open the shutters. I
supposed he wished to see the light of day, the sun and
God's world for the last time. I pulled back the curtain, but the dawning day was as sad and sorrowful as
the poor, expiring life of the dying man. There was
no sun. Clouds covered the sky with a misty shroud;
it was rainy, louring, sad. A drizzling rain beat against
the windowpanes and washed them down with
streams of cold, dirty water. It was dull and dark. The
rays of pale daylight scarcely penetrated into the room,
barely vying with the flickering light of the icon-lamp.
The dying man looked at me so sadly and shook his
head. The next moment he was dead.

Anna Fyodorovna arranged the funeral herself. A

·ery plain coffin was bought, and a carter was hired. To repay the costs of the funeral, Anna Fyodorovna seized the dead man's books and all his belongings. The old man argued and shouted, took away as many books as he could from her, stuffing his pockets and even filling his hat with them. He carried them about for the next three days and did not part from them even when it was time for him to go to church. All this time he seemed to be in a sort of frenzy. He kept bustling about the coffin with a strange kind of solicitude, adjusting the paper ribbon with its sacred images on the forehead of his dead son and lighting or snuffing the candles. It was clear that his thoughts could not remain fixed for a moment on any subject. Neither my mother nor Anna Fyodorovna were present at the church service. My mother was ill, and Anna Fyodorovna was all set to go when she had a violent quarrel with old Pokrovsky and stayed at home. Only the old man and I were there. During the service I was seized by a certain panic, as though by a premonition of the future. I could scarcely remain standing through the service. At last the coffin was closed, nailed down, put on the cart, and taken away. I accompanied it only as far as the end of the street. The driver broke into a trot. The old man ran after him weeping loudly, his sobs breaking and trembling as he ran after the cart. The poor man lost his hat but did not stop to retrieve it. His head was wet with the rain, the wind was rising, and the sleet lashed and stung his face. The old fellow did not seem to feel anything as he ran sobbing from one side of the cart to the other. The skirt of his threadbare coat flapped about in the wind like a pair of wings. Books protruded from his pockets, in his arms he carried a huge volume which he clasped tightly. Passers-by took off their hats and crossed themselves. Some of them stopped and gazed in astonishment at the poor old man. Every now and then books would fall from his pockets into the mud. People would stop to draw his attention to his loss. He would pick up a book and once more dash off in pursuit of the cart. At the corner of the street some old beggar woman insisted on accompanying him to the cemetery. At last the cart turned a corner and disappeared from my sight. I went home and threw myself into a paroxysm of grief on my mother's breast. I clasped her tightly, tightly in my arms, kissed her, burst into sobs, clinging to her fearfully as though in an effort to hold in my embrace my last friend and save her from death. . . . But already death was standing over my poor mother! . . .

. . . . . .

June 11th.

Thank you so much for our walk to the Islands yesterday! How fresh and beautiful and how green everything is there! I had not seen anything green for such a long time. During my illness I kept thinking that I would never get better, that I was going to die for certain, that I had to die! You can, therefore, imagine my feelings yesterday. You are not angry with me for being so sad yesterday, are you? I was very happy yesterday, but, somehow, I always feel sad in my happiest moments. It is true I cried, but that is nothing. I don't know myself why I cry. I'm afraid I can't help feeling irritable and morbid. All my impressions are morbid. The pale, cloudless sky, the sunset, the serene evening—all that—I don't know why but I could not help reacting to everything so poignantly and so painfully that my heart overflowed and my soul begged for tears. But why am I writing all this to you? It is difficult to explain it to one's own heart, but it is even more difficult to explain it to someone else. But possibly you may see what I mean. Laughter and sadness! How good you are, Mr. Devushkin! Yesterday you kept looking into my eyes to read there what I was feeling and you were so delighted by my enthusiasm. A shrub, an avenue, a stretch of water—and there you were standing before me, preening yourself, gazing into my eyes as though you were showing me your own possessions. This shows what a good heart you have. That is why I am fond of you. Well, goodbye. Today I am not feeling well again. I got my feet wet yesterday and caught a cold. Theodora isn't feeling too well, either. So we are both sick now. Do not forget me. Come and see me more often.

Your
B.D.

June 12th.

My darling Barbara,

I had thought, dear heart, that you were going to describe everything that happened yesterday in verse, but all you did was to write only one little page. I'm saying this because though you did not write a lot to me in your page, you described it all very beautifully and sweetly. Nature, all sorts of rural scenes, and the rest about feelings—all that you described very beautifully. I'm afraid I have no such talent. I may scribble a score of pages, but nothing comes of it. I can't describe anything properly. I have tried, you see. You write, my dear, that I am a good man who bears no malice, who is incapable of hurting anyone, and who appreciates God's goodwill to men as expressed in the beauties of nature, and, in short, you overwhelm me with all sorts of praises. All that may very well be true, dear heart, it may well be perfectly true. I am indeed, as you say and I know it myself. But, though, after reading what you've written, I can't help feeling deeply touched, all sorts of painful thoughts steal into my mind afterwards. Listen, dear heart, I have something to tell you.

I will begin from the time when I joined the civil service. I was only seventeen, and now it will soon be thirty years since I entered on my career as a government official. Well, all I can say is that I have worn out quite a lot of uniforms. I grew up to man's estate. I grew wiser. I've observed the ways of men. I've lived, I may say, I've lived so irreproachably that at one time there was even a chance of my being presented with a decoration. You may not believe that, but I assure you I'm not telling a lie. But, I'm afraid, dear heart, wicked people prevented that. I don't mind telling you, my dear, that though I may be a man of no importance, a foolish man, perhaps, I have feelings like any other man. Well, do you know, my darling, what wicked men did to me? I am ashamed to say it. You'd better ask why they did it. Well, they did it because I am a quiet sort of fellow, because I am meek, because I am good-natured. They did not like me so they started on me. . . . It began by all sorts of innuendoes. "You, Mr. Devushkin, are—er—this or that. . . ." Then it went on: "Why trouble to ask Devushkin at all!" And how they just conclude with: "Well, it's Devushkin, of course!" So, you see, dear heart, how it turned out in the end: it's all Devushkin's fault! All they achieved was to make Devushkin into a by-word in the whole of our department. And not only did they make me into a by-word and almost into a word of abuse, they went so far as to find fault with my boots, with my uniform, with my hair. Nothing was to their taste, everything had to be changed. And all that has been going on every day since time immemorial. I have got used to it. I get used to everything because I am a peaceful man, an unimportant man. But all the same, why all this? Have I done any harm to anyone? Have I got promotions at the expense of anyone? Have I cast a slur on anyone before our superiors? Asked for a raise in salary? Engaged in some conspiracy? Have I? Why, you'd do me an injustice if you even thought of it. What do I want it all for? Why, my dear, just think: do I possess the abilities for such acts of perfidy and ambition? Why, then, all these attacks on me, for goodness' sake? You don't regard me as a man worthy of respect, do you, and you, dear heart, are far better than any of them. For what is the greatest social virtue? In a private conversation the other day, Eustaphy Ivanovich remarked to me that the most important social virtue is the knack of making a lot of money. He was joking, of course (I know he was joking), but the moral is that no one should be a burden on anyone, and I am no burden on anybody! I eat my own crust of bread, an ordinary crust, it is true, sometimes a dry one, but it is one obtained by my own exertions and put to lawful and irreproachable use. Well, what's to be done about it? I realise only too well that I do not do a great deal by copying official documents, but I am proud of it, nevertheless: I am working, earning a living by the sweat of my brow. After all, what's wrong about copying official documents? It's not a sin, is it? "He's just a copy clerk! An office clerk who copies documents!" What's so dishonourable about that? My handwriting is legible, neat, pleasant to look at, and His Excellency is satisfied. I am copying the most important documents for him. There is no *style* about it, I know that myself. I know it lacks style, damn it! That's why I have never got on in the service, and even to you, my dear, I write simply, without flourishes, whatever thought happens to strike me at the moment. I know it all, but then if everyone became a writer, who'd be a copyist? That's the question I'd like you to answer, dear heart. Well anyway, I realise now that I am needed, that I am indispensable, and that a man cannot be thrown off his balance by some such trifle. All right, let me be a drudge, if they think the cap fits. But this drudge is wanted, this drudge is of some use. Drudges like that are valued, drudges like that are awarded decorations —that's the sort of drudge I am! However, enough of that, my dear. I didn't really want to talk about it, but I'm afraid I got a little carried away. Still, it is pleasant to do justice to oneself occasionally. Good-bye, my own, my darling, my dear little comforter. I'll most certainly come to see you, come to see how you are, my only one. In the meantime do not worry. I'll bring you a book. Well, good-bye, darling Barbara.

Your sincere well-wisher,
Makar Devushkin.

June 20th.

Dear Mr. Devushkin,

I am writing to you in a hurry. I'm trying to get my work finished in time. You see, the point is there is the chance of a bargain. Theodora says that she knows someone who wishes to sell a civil servant's uniform, which is practically new, as well as underwear, a waistcoat and a cap, very cheaply, too, she says. Why shouldn't you buy it? You're not hard up now and you have some money to spare. You told me so yourself. Please, don't deny yourself. You must have it. Just think what old clothes you walk about in. Disgraceful! They're all in patches. You have no new clothes—I know that, though you tell me you have. Goodness knows what you did with them. So listen to me, please, and buy it. Do it for my sake. Buy it if you love me.

You have sent me some lingeries as a present. But, look here, my dear Mr. Devushkin, you are ruining yourself. Heavens, think of the money you have spent on me already—such a terrible lot of money! Oh, you do like to throw money about, don't you? I don't need it. It was quite unnecessary. I know, I am quite sure that you love me. It's quite unnecessary to remind me of it by presents. It's hard for me to accept them from you, for I know how much they must have cost you. Once and for all—do you hear?—it's enough! I beg you, I implore you. You ask me, dear Mr. Devushkin, to send you a continuation of my journal. You want me to finish it. I don't know how I managed to write even what I had written. I don't know if I have the strength now to write about my past. I do not want even to think of it. I'm terrified of those memories. Most painful of all is it to speak of my poor mother who left her poor child a prey to those monsters. My blood runs cold at the very thought of it. It's all still so fresh in my mind. I've hardly had time to dismiss it from my thoughts, let alone to compose myself, though a year has passed since it all happened. But you know it all, don't you?

I have told you of Anna Fyodorovna's present ideas. She accuses me of ingratitude and denies that she is working against me with Mr. Bykov. She keeps sending for me and telling me that I am begging for crumbs and that I'm following the wrong road. She says that if I return to her, she'll settle the matter with Mr. Bykov and will have him redress the wrong he did me. She says Mr. Bykov wants to give me a dowry. I don't want anything to do with them. I am quite happy here with you and my kind Theodora, whose devotion reminds me of my old nurse. You may be only a distant relative of mine, but you protect me by your name. I don't know anything about them and I shall try to forget them if I can. What more do they want of me? Theodora says that it's all empty talk and that they'll leave me in peace in time. God grant they do!

B.D.

June 21st.

My darling, dear heart,

I want to write to you but I don't know how to begin. You must admit, dear heart, that the way you and I are living now is strange. I'm saying this because never before have I spent such happy days. It's just as though the good Lord had blessed me with a home and a family of my own. My dearest, darling, my beautiful one, why mention the four silly chemises I sent you? You needed them, didn't you? I found out from Theodora herself. Why, dear heart, it makes me particularly happy to gratify you. It gives me great pleasure and please, leave me to enjoy it. Let me be and don't try to stop me. I've never experienced anything like that, dear heart. Why, I move in the best circles now. I lead a double life. First, because, to my delight, you live so very close to me, and, secondly, a lodger here, a neighbour of mine, Ratazyaev, invited me to tea today! He's a retired civil servant who gives literary parties. This evening they're having one of their meetings. We shall read literature. That's the sort of fellow I am now, dear heart,—yes indeed! Well, good-bye now. You see, I've written all this without any particular aim and solely to tell you about my good fortune. You have let me know through Theodora, my darling, that you need some coloured silk for embroidery. I'll buy it, dear heart, I'll buy you the silk. To-morrow I shall have the pleasure of finally satisfying your wish. I know the very place where I can buy it. And now let me remain

> Your most sincere friend,
> *Makar Devushkin.*

June 22nd.

Dear Barbara,

I have to inform you, my dear, that a most sad event has taken place in our house, an event truly, truly worthy of pity. Today, about five o'clock in the morning, Gorshkov's little son died. I'm afraid I don't know what he died of, scarlet fever or something, goodness only knows. I have just paid a visit to the

Gorshkovs. Dear me, how poor they are! And what disorder! No wonder: the whole family lives in one room, partitioned off only by a screen for decency's sake. Already, there's a little coffin there—a very plain coffin, but rather nice; they bought it ready-made; their boy was about nine, promised well, they told me. What a pitiful sight, my dear. The mother is not crying, but she looks so heart-broken, the poor woman. It may well be a relief for them to have one burden less on their shoulders; they have two children left, a baby and a little girl of over six. Some pleasure it must be to see a child suffering, your own child, too, and be unable to help him! The father, wearing an old, greasy frock-coat was sitting on a broken chair. Tears rolled down his cheeks, perhaps not so much from grief, but because of his bad eyes. What a queer fellow he is! Always blushes when you talk to him, looks confused and doesn't know what to say to you. The little girl, his daughter, was leaning against the coffin, the poor thing, so sad and thoughtful. I'm afraid, dear heart, I do not like to see a child lost in thought—an unpleasant sight! On the floor beside her lay a rag doll, but she was not playing with it; she stood there with a finger to her lips—motionless. Our landlady gave her a sweet; she took it but was not eating it. Sad, dear Barbara, isn't it?

Makar Devushkin.

June 25th.

Dear Mr. Devushkin,

I'm returning you your book. What a horrible book! I wouldn't touch it. Where did you dig this precious thing up? Joking apart, do you really like such books?

The other day I was promised something to read. I'll let you have it, too, if you like. Good-bye for the present. I really am too busy to write any more.

B.D.

June 26th.

Dear Barbara,

You see, I really have not read that book myself, dear heart. I mean, I just browsed through it and I saw that it was a lot of nonsense, only written to make people laugh. So I thought that it must really be funny and that dear Barbara might like it. That's why I sent it to you. Anyway, Ratazyaev promised to give me something really literary to read, so you will soon have your books, dear heart. Ratazyaev knows about these things—he's an authority; writes himself. Goodness me, indeed he does! A facile writer and a fine stylist. I mean, you can see it in every word he utters, in the most ordinary, common word, such as I might sometimes use in talking to Faldoni or Teresa, there's style even there. I go to his literary parties. We smoke our pipes, and he reads to us, keeps it up he does, till five o'clock in the morning, and we all listen to him. It's sheer delight—not just literature. Beautiful—flowers, simply flowers—a bunch of flowers on every page! He's so urbane, too. Good-natured, pleasant. What am I compared to him? Nothing. He's a man with a reputation, and what am I? Why, I don't exist at all! Yet, he is well disposed towards me. I am copying things out for him. But you mustn't think that it's a trick, I mean that the reason he is so well disposed towards me is that I am copying his things. Don't believe such stories, dear heart, don't believe such base stories. Not at all. I'm doing it of my own free will, I volunteered to do it, I'm doing it because I want to please him. If he is well disposed towards me, it's because he wants to please me. I appreciate the delicacy of his action, dear heart. He is a good, a very good man and a superb writer.

Literature is such an excellent thing, Barbara, such an excellent thing. I found that out from him the other day. A profound thing! It fortifies the hearts of men, it's instructive and—all sorts of things of a similar nature are written about it in his book. Beautifully written! Literature is a picture, I mean, a certain sort of picture, and a mirror. A medium for the expression of passions, for the most subtle criticism, a lesson in morals, and a document. I gleaned it all from them. To tell you the truth, dear heart, there I am, sitting with them and listening to them (and, perhaps, also smoking a pipe like them), but when they start some violent argument about all sorts of different matters, I simply give up—and I daresay, dear heart, you and I would just have to give up. In their company I'm just a stupid idiot, ashamed of myself, all evening trying hard to put something into words of my own so as to take part in the general discussion, but the words just aren't there! You can't help being sorry for yourself, dear Barbara, I mean that you're not quite up to it—or, as the proverb has it, you are grown up in years but not in wisdom. Why, what do I do in my spare time now? I sleep like a silly fool. Well, instead of useless sleeping, I could have done something pleasant, I mean, I could have sat down to write something. Useful to oneself and good for others. Good heavens, dear heart, see how much money they get, the Lord forgive

them! Ratazyaev for instance—the money he rakes in!
To write a sheet is child's play to him. Why, sometimes he writes five a day and, he says, he takes three
hundred roubles for a sheet. A little anecdote, say, on
something of interest—five hundred, and you jolly
well have to pay, whether you like it or not, and
sometimes—well—we'll pocket a thousand! What do
you say to that, Miss Dobroselov? And that's not all.
He has a bookful of poems, short poems, all of them,
and he asks seven thousand for them—seven thousand,
just think! Why, it's real estate, a big house! He tells
me he was offered five thousand, but he refused it. I
tried to reason with him. "Accept the five thousand
from them and to hell with them," I pleaded. "Why,
five thousand is good money!" "No, no," he said.
"They will give me seven thousand, the rascals!" A
cunning customer!

Well, dear heart, having gone so far, I may as well
quote you a passage from *Italian Passions*. That is the
title of one of his works. Read it my dear, and judge
for yourself.

"Vladimir gave a violent start and the passions
welled up madly in him, and his blood reached boiling
point.

" 'Countess,' he cried, 'Countess, do you realise how
terrible this passion of mine is? How boundless this
madness? No, my dreams have not deceived me! I love
you ecstatically, insanely, frenziedly! All your husband's blood would not quench the fierce, surging
rapture of my soul. No trivial obstacles will quell the
all-consuming, hellish fire that churns up my exhausted breast. Oh, Zinaida, Zinaida!'

" 'Vladimir,' whispered the Countess, beside herself, sinking on his chest.

"A sigh escaped from his breast. A conflagration blazed up in a bright flame on the altar of love and seared the breasts of the unhappy sufferers.

" 'Vladimir!' whispered the Countess in ecstasy. Her bosom heaved, her cheeks glowed, her eyes burned. . . .

"A new, terrible union was consummated. . . .

"Half an hour later the old Count entered his wife's boudoir.

" 'Don't you think, darling,' he said, patting his wife's cheek, 'we ought to ask our dear guest to stay to tea?' "

Well, dear heart, let me ask you what you think of that. True, it's a little too outspoken, no doubt about that, but it's good, don't you think? Yes, it's excellent, quite excellent. Here's another extract from his story *Yermak and Zuleika* I'd like to copy out for you.

First imagine, dear heart, that the Cossack Yermak, the savage and fierce conqueror of Siberia, is in love with Zuleika, the daughter of the Siberian King Kuchum, whom he keeps prisoner. An event from the times of Ivan the Terrible, as you see. Here's a dialogue between Yermak and Zuleika.

" 'You love me, Zuleika. Oh, repeat it, repeat it!'

" 'I love you, Yermak,' whispered Zuleika.

" 'Heaven and earth I thank you! I am happy. You've given me all, all my troubled spirit has been seeking since the days of my boyhood. So that's where you have led me, oh, my guiding star, that's why you brought me here, beyond the Stone Belt! I shall now show my Zuleika to the whole world, and people, those mad monsters, will not dare to accuse me. Oh, if only they would understand those mysterious sufferings of her tender heart! Oh, if only they were able to see a whole poem in one little tear of my Zuleika! Oh, let me dry that tear with my kisses, let me drink it, that heavenly tear—oh, unearthly one!'

" 'Yermak,' said Zuleika, 'the world is evil, men are unjust. They will persecute us, they will condemn us, my dear Yermak. What will a poor maiden, reared amid her native snows of Siberia in the tent of her father, do in your cold, icy, soulless, selfish world? People will not understand me, my darling, my sweetheart!'

" 'Then a Cossack sabre will soar and whistle over their heads!' cried Yermak, rolling his eyes wildly."

You can imagine, dear Barbara, what Yermak felt when he learned that his Zuleika had been murdered. The blind old Kuchum, taking advantage of the darkness of the night, had, in Yermak's absence, stolen into his tent and stabbed his own daughter, thinking that he was dealing a fatal blow to Yermak, who had robbed him of his crown and sceptre.

" 'I love to scrape iron against a stone!' cried Yermak, wild with fury, as he sharpened his steel knife on a Shaman's stone. 'I want their blood, their blood! They must be tortured, tortured, tortured!!!' "

Then Yermak, unable to survive the loss of his Zuleika, throws himself into the Irtysh, and that is the end of the story.

Well, and here, for instance, is another small extract in a humorously descriptive vein, written to make people laugh:

"Do you know Ivan Prokofyevich Zholtopuz? I

mean the man who bit the leg of Prokofy Ivanovich. Ivan Prokofyevich is a man of a violent temper, but of rare virtues; Prokofy Ivanovich, on the other hand, is extremely fond of radishes and honey. It all happened at the time Pelageya Antonovna knew him. Do you know Pelageya Antonovna? I mean, the woman who always puts on her skirts inside out. . . ."

Why, Barbara, it's killingly funny, simply killingly funny! We split our sides with laughter when he read it to us. What a man! I must admit, dear heart, it may be a little bit too ingenious and certainly too playful, but quite innocent, without the slightest hint of free-thinking or liberal ideas. Let me observe, dear heart, that Ratazyaev is a man of excellent conduct as well as a first-class writer, which is more than can be said for other writers.

But really—I mean, I sometimes can't help thinking: what if I were to write something? . . . What would happen then? Let us assume, for instance, that for no reason at all a book were suddenly to make its appearance in the world under the title: *Poems by Makar Devushkin!* What would you have said then, my little angel? What would you have imagined or thought then? So far as I'm concerned, dear heart, I can truly say that as soon as my book appeared in print, I'd most certainly be unable to summon up enough courage to show my face on Nevsky Avenue. For you can imagine what I would feel like to have people say: here comes the great writer and poet, Devushkin. . . . Yes, it is Devushkin himself! I mean, what on earth would I be able to do with, for instance, these boots of mine? For I must tell you in passing, dear heart, that they are covered in patches and, to tell the truth, the soles sometimes come off in a most indecent fashion. Can you imagine what people would say if they knew that the writer Devushkin walked about in patched boots? If some duchess or countess knew, what would she say? Mind you, she might not have noticed it, for I don't think countesses are interested in boots and certainly not boots worn by civil servants (for, you see, there are boots and boots), but she would have been told about it. Why, my own friends would have betrayed me. Ratazyaev would have been the first to betray me: he goes to see Countess V., and, he says, she treats him like one of the family. She's a darling, he says, a literary lady. A damn clever chap, that Ratazyaev!

But enough of this. I write all this, my angel, just for fun, to amuse you. Good-bye, my darling. I'm afraid I've scribbled a lot for you, but that's really because I am in high spirits today. We've just had dinner at Ratazyaev's, all of us (they are gay dogs, dear heart), and we had such drinks. . . . But why write to you about that? Only please, dear Barbara, don't think the worse of me because of that. I don't mean any harm really. I'll send you the books. I shall indeed. A novel by Paul de Kock seems to be very popular, but I don't think, dear heart, Paul de Kock is quite. . . . No, of course not. Paul de Kock is not fit for you. They say about him, dear heart, that he throws all the Petersburg critics into a state of righteous indignation. I am sending you a pound of sweets —bought it specially for you. Eat them, darling, and every time you have one, remember me. Only don't bite fruit drops. Just suck them or they'll make your teeth ache. Do you like crystallized fruits? Write and

tell me. Well, good-bye, good-bye. Christ be with you,
my darling. And I shall always remain

Your most faithful friend,
Makar Devushkin.

June 27th.

Dear Mr. Devushkin,

Theodora says that I have only to express a wish
and some people will be glad to help me and obtain
an excellent job for me as governess in a certain house.
What do you think, my friend? Shall I accept it, or
not? Of course, I should no longer be a burden to you
then, and the post, too, seems to be well paid. On the
other hand, I can't help feeling terrified of going to
live in a strange house. They are apparently landown-
ers. They'll start finding out things about me, asking
questions, getting curious. What can I tell them? Besides, I am such an unsociable creature. I'm so shy:
I like to live in a place I'm accustomed to. Somehow
one is happier in a place one is used to. You may be
hard up, but still you are happier. Besides, I should
have to have money for moving to my new quarters,
and goodness only knows what my duties would be.
I may simply have to be a children's nursemaid. The
people don't seem to me to be very good, either: they
have changed their governess three times in two years.
Please, dear Mr. Devushkin, let me know what you
think: shall I go or not? Why don't you ever come to
see me now? I only see you for a moment, and that,
too, very seldom. Almost always on a Sunday in church.
What an unsociable man you are, to be sure! Just like
me. And yet I am practically a relation of yours. You
don't love me, and I feel so depressed sometimes when

I am alone. Many a time, especially at dusk, I feel so terribly lonely. Theodora has gone out somewhere and I am left alone in my room, thinking, thinking, remembering the past, its joys and sorrows. It all passes before my eyes, rising fitfully as though out of a mist. Familiar faces appear (I almost begin to see them as though they were actually beside me). I see my mother most of all. Oh, if you knew what dreams I have! I feel that my health is getting worse; I am so weak; when I got up this morning, I felt sick and I have such a bad cough. I feel, I know, that I shall die soon. Who will bury me? Who will follow my coffin? Who will be sorry for me? And now I may have to die among strangers in a strange place, in a strange house. Dear God, how sad life is! Why do you, my dear friend, keep feeding me on sweets? I'm sure I don't know where you get all the money. Dear friend, please take care of your money, take care of your money, for God's sake. Theodora is selling a rug I have made. People are offering fifty roubles for it, which I think is very good. I didn't think I'd get so much for it. I'll give ten roubles to Theodora and make myself a dress, a plain, warm dress. I'll make you a waistcoat, make it myself and I'll choose good material for it.

Theodora got me a book—*The Tales of Belkin*—which I'll send you if you would care to read it. Only, please, do not dirty it and do not keep it too long: it does not belong to me. It is by Pushkin. Two years ago I read these stories with my mother and now I feel too sad to read them again. If you have any books, send them to me, but only so long as you have not got them from Ratazyaev. I expect he'll give you one of his books, if indeed he has published anything. How can you like his work, Mr. Devushkin? It's such rubbish! Well, good-bye. I have been chattering away, haven't I? When I'm feeling sad, I like to chatter about anything under the sun. It's a sort of medicine: I feel much better at once, but especially if I can unburden myself. Good-bye, good-bye, my friend.

Yours

B.D.

June 28th.

My darling Barbara,

Away with depression! You ought to be ashamed of yourself. Come, come, my angel, how can you allow such thoughts to enter your head? You're not ill, darling. Not at all. You're blooming, indeed you are! A little pale, perhaps, but you're still blooming. And what's all this about your dreams and visions? Fie—for shame, darling! Take no notice of those dreams—simply take no notice of them. Why do I sleep so well? Why am I not upset by anything? Just look at me, dear heart. I live well, I sleep peacefully, there's nothing the matter with my health, I'm in fine fettle —a sight for the gods! Come, come, for shame, darling, no more of this. I know that little head of yours —the moment something happens you start imagining things and feeling miserable. Stop it for my sake, sweetheart. Take a job as a menial? Never! No and no again! What makes you think of such a thing? What's the matter with you? To move from your home, too! No, dear heart, I shan't allow it, I shall fight against such an intention with might and main. I'll sell my old frock-coat and walk the streets in my shirt rather than let you want. No, darling, no! But, then, I know you! It's just a whim, a whim, pure and simple! The truth is that it's all Theodora's fault; the silly old woman must have suggested it to you. Don't believe her, dear heart. But, I suppose, you don't know anything, do you, dear heart? She's a silly, shrewish, cantankerous woman. Why, she drove her husband into his grave! Or has she by any chance got on your nerves? No, no, dear heart, not for anything in the world! What will happen to me then? What will then be left for me to do? No, darling Barbara, put that idea right out of your head. What do you lack here? I dote on you, you are fond of me, well, then, live as quietly as you wish, sew or read, or perhaps do not sew—it really makes no difference, only do not leave me. Just imagine what it will be like if you do go away. I'll get you books and later on, perhaps go for another walk in the country. Only, please, please, dear heart, try to think clearly and do not get silly ideas into your head because of some trifles. I shall come and see you, and that as soon as possible, only first you must let me tell you quite frankly and openly: you're wrong, darling, you're wrong! Of course, I'm not an educated man. I'm aware of that. I was too poor to get a good education. But that's not what I'm driving at. It's not me I'm concerned about. It's Ratazyaev. Say what you like, I must stand up for him. He's a friend of mine, and that's why I must stand up for him. He's an excellent writer, an excellent, excellent writer. Yes, indeed, an excellent writer. I don't agree with you, and never shall. He writes in a flowery style, laconically, figuratively, and he has all sorts of ideas: first-class! You must have read him without sympathy, darling, or perhaps you were not in the right mood when you read him, angry with Theodora about something, or, perhaps something else happened to upset you. No, no, read him with sympathy, when you're feeling better, when you are happy and contented and in a pleasant frame of mind, when, for instance, you've got a sweet in your mouth—you read him then! I'm quite willing to admit (who is not?) that there are better writers than Ratazyaev, far better writers indeed, but they are good and Ratazyaev is good, too; they write well, and he writes well. He is different from anyone else, he writes to please himself, and he does well to go on writing like that. Well, good-bye, dear heart. I can't write any more. I am in a hurry. There's something I have to do. Now, please, dear heart, dearest darling, do not worry, and may the Lord be with you, and I remain

Your faithful friend,
Makar Devushkin.

P.S. Thank you for the book, my dear. I'll read Pushkin, too; this evening I shall most certainly come and see you.

July 1st.

My dear Mr. Devushkin,

No, no, my friend, I shall never be happy living near you. I have changed my mind and I find that it is very wrong of me to refuse so good a post. Then I should at least not have to worry about my daily bread; I'd do my best to earn the kindness of strangers and even try to change my character, if necessary. It is true it is distressing and hurtful to live among strangers and to ingratiate oneself with people you do not know, to dissemble and force oneself, but God

will help me. I can't very well remain a recluse forever. I have had similar experiences before. I remember the time when as a little girl I used to go to
boarding-school. On Sundays, I used to spend the time
at home playing and romping about. Sometimes my
mother would scold me, but it did not matter, for
I felt happy and gay. Yet as evening approached, I
would suddenly feel terribly sad, for at nine o'clock
the next day I had to go back to school where everything was strange and cold and strict, where on Mon-
days the mistresses were cross and bad-tempered. I
was so depressed that I felt like crying. I would retire
to a corner and weep, all by myself, trying to conceal
my tears for fear that they might say I was lazy. But
it was not because I had to do any lessons that I used
to cry. Well, in time I got used to things and later,
when I left the boarding-school, I also cried when saying good-bye to my schoolfriends. Besides it is wrong
of me to be a burden on you both. The thought is
torture to me. I tell you this frankly because I am
used to being frank with you. Can't I see that Theodora gets up ever so early every day to do the washing
she has taken in and keeps on working till late at night
—a woman of her age who needs rest so badly? Can't
I see that you are ruining yourself because of me, saving your last copeck so that you can spend it on me?
You can't afford it, my friend. You write that you'd
rather sell everything you have than leave me in want.
I believe you, my friend, I believe in your good heart.
But you say that now when you have received some
unexpected sum of money, now when you have received a gratuity, but what will happen later? You
know very well that I am always ill, that I cannot work

as you do, though I'd be glad to. Besides I cannot always get work. What, then, am I to do? Worry myself to death watching you two? How can I possibly be of any use to you? And why am I so necessary to you, dear friend? What good have I done you? I am attached to you with all my soul, I love you dearly, strongly, with all my heart, but—such is my cruel lot! —I know how to love and I can love, but that is all—I cannot do good, I cannot repay you for all your benefactions. Do not, therefore, keep me any longer, reflect carefully and tell me what you really think.

In expectation of which,

I remain,

Your loving,

B.D.

July 1st.

Nonsense, nonsense, dearest Barbara, sheer nonsense! Leave you like that and goodness only knows what ideas you may get in your little head. This is bad and that is bad! But I can see now that it's all nonsense. What is it that you miss so much? Tell me that. Here we love you, you love us, we are all happy and contented—what more do you want? What will you do among strangers? I don't suppose you realise what strangers are like. You'd better ask me and I'll tell you what strangers are like. I know, dear heart, I know them well. They're evil, Barbara, so evil that however much you try to please them, they'll worry the life out of you by their reproaches, their taunts and their black looks. You are snug and warm here just as if you were sheltered in a nest. Besides, if you left us, we'd be left stranded. What could we do with-

out you? What could I, an old man, do then? We don't
need you? You're of no use to us? What do you mean?
No, dear heart, I think you can judge for yourself
whether you are useful or not. You're certainly very
useful to me, my dear. You have such a beneficial influence on me. . . . I'm thinking of you now and I
feel happy. . . . Every time I write you a letter I give
you an account of all my feelings and receive detailed
answers from you. . . . I have bought you a wardrobe,
had a bonnet made for you. . . . Whenever you want
me to do something, I do it. . . . How can you say
you are not useful? Why, what should I do if left alone
in my old age? Of what use should I be? You haven't
thought of that, have you, Barbara? You'd better
think of it. I mean, of what use would I be without
you? I have got used to you, my dear. What would
happen if you were to go away? Why I'd go and drown
myself in the Neva. Yes, indeed, I would. Why, my
darling, do you really want me to be carted off to the
Volnovo Cemetery, with some shuffling old beggar
woman following my coffin, and the grave-digger covering it with earth and going off and leaving me there.
It's not right, dear heart, not right at all. Indeed, not.
I'm returning you your book, dear friend, Barbara, and
if you should ask me what I think of it, I'd say that I'd
never read such a wonderful book in all my life. I keep
asking myself, dear heart, how I could have remained
such a blockhead until now, the Lord forgive me.
What have I ever done? From what wilds did I come?
You see, dear heart, I know nothing. Simply nothing.
Let me tell you quite frankly, dearest Barbara, I am
an uneducated man. I've read little until now, very

little, practically nothing. *Portrait of Man*,[1] quite a clever work, I have read; *The Boy who Played Various Tunes on Bells*,[2] I have read; and *The Cranes of Ibycus*.[3] That's all. I have not read anything else. Now I've also read *The Station Master* in your book. Let me tell you, dear heart, it can happen that you go through life without knowing that under your very nose there is a book in which your life is described in the minutest detail. What you have never even noticed before, you gradually remember, as you start reading such a book, and find out and discover. There's one more reason that I liked your book: some books you read and read and you can't make head or tail of them, however much you try. It is so damn clever that you can't understand a word of it. Take me, for instance. I'm slow-witted, I'm slow-witted by nature, and I can't read works that are a little too grand. But you read a book like that and you feel as though you had written it yourself, just as though— how shall I put it?—as though you had taken possession of your own heart—whatever it might be—had turned it inside out for people to see, and described it all in detail—that's how it is! And how simple it is, good Lord! Why, I could have written it myself! Why, indeed, shouldn't I have written it myself? You see, I feel the same, just like the people in the book. Indeed, I sometimes find myself in the same situations as, for instance, that poor old Samson Vyrin. How many poor wretches like Samson Vyrin are walking

[1] A didactic treatise by Alexander Galich, one of Pushkin's tutors at the Petersburg Lycée, published in 1834.
[2] A novel by Ducray-Duminil, dealing with the adventures of a poor boy, a street musician, who becomes a rich philanthropist.
[3] A ballad by Friedrich Schiller translated by Vasili Zhukovsky.

about among us? And how cleverly it is all described! I nearly burst into tears, dear heart, when I read that the poor fellow took to drink, lost his memory, became embittered and took to lying about, sleeping all day long under his sheepskin coat, drowning his sorrows with punch, crying bitterly, wiping his eyes with the dirty skirt of his coat, as he thought of his stray lamb, his daughter Dunyasha. Yes, that is natural! Read it—it is natural! It lives! I have seen it myself—it's happening all around me. Take Teresa—but why go so far—take our poor civil servant—why, he is perhaps just the same kind of man as Samson Vyrin except that his surname, Gorshkov, is different. It's the sort of thing that can happen to anyone—you as well as me. It might even happen to some count who lives on Nevsky Avenue or on the embankment, except that it might appear to be different, for people like that have their own style of living, something on a higher level, but the same thing can happen to him, too, as well as to me. That's how it is, dear heart, and you want to go away and leave me. Why, if you were to do that, anything might happen to me. You might ruin both yourself and me. For heaven's sake, my darling, get rid of those airy ideas and don't torture me for nothing. Really, how could you possibly provide for yourself, my poor little unfledged nestling, how could you avoid utter ruin or defend yourself against evildoers? Think it over, dearest, get better and don't listen to foolish advice and calumny. Read your book again, read it carefully: it will do you a lot of good.

I have spoken to Ratazyaev about *The Station Master.* He said it is all old-fashioned and that now books are published with illustrations and all sorts of cap-

tions. But I really could not make head or tail of what
he was saying. He concluded by declaring that Pushkin was all right, that he had brought glory to Holy
Russia, and a lot more to that effect about him. Yes,
it was all very nice, Barbara, very nice. Read the book
again with attention, follow my advice, and leave an
old man happy by your obedience. Then the Lord
God himself will reward you, my dear. He will most
certainly reward you.

Your true friend,
Makar Devushkin.

July 6th.

Dear Mr. Devushkin,

Today Theodora brought me fifteen roubles. The
poor woman was so glad when I gave her three roubles. I am writing to you in haste. I am now cutting
out the waistcoat for you. Lovely material—yellow
with a pattern of flowers. I am sending you a book of
miscellaneous stories, some of which I have read myself. Read one of them. It is called: *The Overcoat.*
You ask me to go to the theatre with you—won't it be
too expensive? We might, of course, go to the gallery.
It's ages since I went to a theatre. I can't remember
when I was there last. But, again, I am wondering if
it wouldn't be too expensive an amusement. Theodora
keeps shaking her head. She says you've taken to living
above your means. I can see that myself. Think how
much money you have spent on me! Take care you
don't get yourself into trouble, my friend. Theodora
was telling me about some rumours of an argument
you are supposed to have had with your landlady about
not paying your rent. I am very worried about you.

Well, good-bye. I'm in a hurry. I have some small matter to see to: fastening ribbons on my bonnet.

B.D.

P.S. If we go to the theatre, I think I'll put on my new bonnet and wear my black cloak. Will that be all right?

July 7th.

Dear Miss Dobroselov,

. . . To resume last night's conversation . . . yes, dear heart, I, too, suffered from the same obsession in the old days. I got infatuated with an actress, fell head over heels in love with her. But that wouldn't have mattered. The remarkable thing was that I had hardly seen her and had only been once in the theatre, and yet I got infatuated with her. Five high-spirited young fellows lived next door to me at the time. I made friends with them, I could not very well have avoided them, though while in their company I never overstepped the borders of decency and decorum. But not to be outdone, I used to agree with them about everything. The things they told me about that actress! Every night, as soon as the theatre doors were opened, the whole gang—they always seemed to have enough money for the things they wanted—the whole gang went to the theatre, to the gallery, and applauded like mad and kept calling that actress—they were simply in a frenzy about her. Later they would not let me go to sleep, all night long they went on talking about her, every one calling her Glasha, every one was in love with her, every one had lost his heart to her. They got me, too, excited about her—defenceless youth that I was (I was very young then). I hardly knew myself how I came to be in the theatre with them, in the fourth row, in the gallery. All I could see was just a corner of the curtain, but I could hear everything. The little actress had indeed a lovely voice—sweet, ringing, nightingale-like. We clapped till our hands ached, we shouted and shouted, in short, we were nearly thrown out. Back at home, I walked about in a daze. I had only one rouble left in my pocket, and next pay-day was a fortnight off! Now, what do you think I did, dear heart? Before going to the office next morning, I called at a French perfumers and spent my whole remaining capital on a bottle of scent and some scented soap. I did not know myself why I bought all that. Nor did I dine at home, but kept walking past her windows. She lived on the fourth floor of a block of flats on Nevsky Avenue. Then I went home, rested for about an hour, and went back to Nevsky Avenue just to go on walking past her windows. I kept it up for six weeks—dangling after her; hired smart cabbies and kept driving past her windows. I became run down, got into debt, and then at last fell out of love with her—got bored! So that's what an actress can reduce a decent fellow to, my dear. Still, I was very young then. Very young. . . .

M.D.

July 8th.

My dear Barbara,

I hasten to return the book which I received from you on the 6th of this month and at the same time I also hasten to put things straight with you in this letter. It is not right, dear heart, it is not right at all that you should have put me in such a difficult position. Let me explain myself, dear heart. It is the Almighty who assigns to every man his station in life—one to wear a general's epaulets, another to serve as a low-grade civil servant; one to give orders, another to carry them out without protest in fear and trembling. All this is determined in accordance with a man's capacity. One may be capable of one thing, another of another, and these capacities are ordained by God himself. I have now been thirty years in the service; I carry out my duties irreproachably, I am abstemious and have never been noted for any disorderly conduct. As a citizen, I freely admit to possessing certain short-comings as well as certain virtues. I am respected by my superiors, and His Excellency himself is satisfied with me, and though he has so far shown me no particular marks of favour, I know that he is satisfied. I have grown old and grey; I am not aware of having done anything I need be ashamed of. Everyone naturally is guilty of some small misdemeanour. No one is without sin, not even you, dear heart. But I have never been accused of any big transgressions or insolent behaviour, I mean, of having done anything against the regulations or in breach of the public peace. I have never been accused of that. That has never happened. Why, I have even been awarded a small honour—but why mention that! You of all people should have known that, dear heart, as he, too, should have known it: having decided to describe it, he must have known about it. No, dear heart, I did not expect this of you. No, dearest, this sort of thing I did not expect of you.

What? Am I not to be allowed to live peacefully after that in my little corner—however poor it may be—without muddying the water, as the proverb has it, without hurting any one, in the fear of God and knowing myself, that no one should hurt me, that no one should break into my hovel to spy on what I am doing in my own home, whether for instance, I possess a decent waistcoat or whether I have all the necessary underwear, whether I have a pair of boots and whether or not they have leather soles, or what I eat and drink, or what I am copying out? What does it matter, dear heart, that where the roadway is bad I sometimes walk on tiptoe to save my boots? Why write of anyone who may sometimes be in such need that he can't afford a cup of tea? Must everybody drink tea? Do I have to look into the mouths of people to see what they are munching? Have I ever offended anyone in this way? No, dear heart, there is no need to offend anyone, if no one interferes with you. Here, Barbara, is an example of what I mean: you go on working zealously and industriously in the service—no trouble!—your superiors respect you (whatever they may think, they still respect you), and then under your very nose and without any visible cause, for no reason at all, someone will spread some disgraceful story about you. It is true, of course, that sometimes you will get yourself something new to wear, and you're so happy you can't sleep, new boots for instance, which you put on with such a feeling of voluptuousness—it's quite true, I felt it myself, for it is pleasant to see your foot in a fine, smart boot—that's well described. But I still cannot help being astonished that Fyodor Fyodorovich should have paid no attention to a book like that and failed to stand up for himself. It is true he is only young, though occupying so important a post, and he sometimes likes to shout, by why shouldn't he shout?

Why shouldn't he haul over the coals some subordi-
nate, if one of us deserves it? And even if he does it
for form's sake—there's nothing wrong about that. If
it is necessary to discipline people, it is necessary to
tell them off, for, between ourselves, Barbara, one of
our fellows will do nothing without being told off,
everyone tries to have his name on some list, to be
able to say you'll find it there or there, but when it
comes to doing something, he does his best to get out
of it. As there are all sorts of grades and each grade
demands its own special kind of reprimand, it is only
natural that the tone of his reprimand should corre-
spond to each grade—that's quite in order! Why, dear
heart, the world is so organised that we turn up our
noses at one another, that each of us tells off someone.
Without that precaution the world could not exist,
and there would be no law and order at all. I really
am astonished that Fyodor Fyodorovich should have
overlooked such an insult. And why write such a thing?
Who wants it? Will any reader give me an overcoat for
it? Or buy me a new pair of boots? No, Barbara, he'll
read it and ask for more. You keep hiding yourself
sometimes, concealing something you haven't done,
afraid to show your face anywhere, for you fear some
slander, for people will spread some scandalous story
about you out of nothing, and, before you know it,
your whole civic and family life is part of literature,
everything has been printed, read, discussed, ridiculed!
Why, soon you won't be able to show yourself in the
street, for everything has been described so well that
one can now recognise any one of us civil servants by
the way he walks! If he had only become better at the
end, had mitigated something, had added, for instance,

after the passage where they threw bits of paper on his head, that for all that he was a good, virtuous citizen who did not deserve such treatment from his friends, who was obedient to his elders (here some example could have been added), wished no evil to anyone, believed in God, and died (if he really wants him to die) honoured by everybody. It would have been better still not to have let the poor man die, but contrive for his overcoat to be found, for the general to find out more about his virtues, get him a job in his office, promote him, raise his salary, so that, you see, virtue would be rewarded and vice punished, and his fellow officials left with nothing. I'd have done it that way, for otherwise what special good is there in that ending? Just an ordinary example from everyday life. How, indeed, could you have sent me such a book, my dear? Why, it's simply not true to life, for such a civil servant could not possibly have existed. Why, my dear, one must lodge a complaint against such a story, lodge a formal complaint.

Your obedient servant,
Makar Devushkin.

July 27th.

My dear Mr. Devushkin,

Your latest news and letters frightened, astonished, and bewildered me, but what Theodora had told me explained everything. But why did you have to despair so greatly and so suddenly to precipitate yourself into such an abyss as you had done? Your explanations did not satisfy me at all. You see, I was quite right, wasn't I, when I insisted on accepting the good post I was offered. Besides, my last experience frightened me in

good earnest. You say that your love for me has forced
you to conceal things from me. I realised that I was
indebted to you for a great many things even when
you kept assuring me that you were spending on me
only the money you had saved up at the bank for some
eventuality. But now that I have learned that you never
had any money and that having by chance heard of
my distress and being moved by it, you decided to
spend on me the salary you had taken in advance and
even sold your clothes when I fell ill, now, having
learned all this, I found myself placed in so painful a
situation that I can't yet make up my mind what to
do or think about it. Oh, Mr. Devushkin, you should
have stopped at your first acts of charity inspired by
sympathy and love for a relative and not gone on
wasting your money on unnecessary things. You have
betrayed our friendship because you have not been
frank with me, and now that I realise that you have
spent your last penny on dresses, chocolates, outings,
the theatre, and books, I pay very dearly for all that
by being sorry for my inexcusable frivolity (for I accepted all these things from you without thinking of
you). All you have done to give me pleasure has turned
into a source of grief for me and left behind it only
useless regret. I saw that you were feeling depressed
lately and though I, too, was expecting something
awful to happen, what has happened now was a complete surprise to me. Why, Mr. Devushkin, you of all
people to have lost heart to such an extent! What will
people think of you now, what will those who know
you say to you? You, whom everyone, including myself, respected for your goodness of heart, your modesty
and your good sense, you have now fallen a victim to

an abominable vice of which you seem never before to have been guilty. You can imagine my state of mind when Theodora informed me that you had been found drunk and incapable in the street and that you had been taken home by the police. I was struck dumb with astonishment, though I had been expecting something unusual to happen because you had disappeared for four days. But has it ever occurred to you what your superiors will say when they find out the true reason for your absence? You say that everyone is laughing at you, that everyone has learned of our relationship and that your neighbours even mention me in their gibes. Pay no attention to this and for God's sake compose yourself. I am also alarmed by the incident between you and those army officers. I have heard rumours about it. Please, tell me what's the meaning of it all? You write that you were afraid to be frank with me, that you were afraid to forfeit my friendship by your confession, that you were in despair at the thought of being unable to help me when I was ill, that you have sold everything to maintain me and prevent me from being sent to the infirmary, that you have borrowed as much as you could, and that you have unpleasant scenes with your landlady every day. But by concealing all this from me, you chose the worse course. Now I know everything. You could not bring yourself to force me to confess that I have been the cause of your unhappy situation and by your conduct now you have redoubled my grief. All this has surprised me. Oh, my friend, misfortune is an infectious illness. The poor and unhappy must avoid each other so as not to increase the infection. I have brought upon you misfortunes such as you had never before expe-

rienced in your humble and solitary life. All this tor-
ments and mortifies me.

Write to me now everything frankly—what has happened to you and what made you do such a thing. Put
my mind at rest if you can. It is not selfishness that
forces me to write about my peace of mind, but my
friendship and love for you, which will never fade from
my heart. Good-bye. I await your answer with impatience. You've had a bad opinion of me, Mr.
Devushkin.

Your sincerely loving,
Barbara Dobroselov.

July 28th.

My precious Barbara,

Now that it is all over and everything is gradually
returning to normal, I can tell you this, dear heart:
you are worried about what people will think of me, to
which I hasten to assure you that my self-respect is
dearer to me than anything else in the world. Therefore, in telling you of my misfortunes and all these
upsets, I am glad to inform you that none of my superiors knows anything about them and will never know
about them, so they will continue to regard me with
the same respect as before. One thing I am afraid of:
I am afraid of gossip. My landlady used to scream, but
now that I have paid her part of the rent with the aid
of the ten roubles you sent me, she only grumbles, and
nothing more. As for the rest, they, too, don't seem to
care. So long as one does not borrow money from
them, they are all right. To conclude my explanations,
let me tell you, dear heart, that I care for your respect
for me more than for anything else in the world and

that I find this a great comfort in my present
troubles. Thank goodness the first shock and the first
predicaments have passed and that you have taken it
in such a way as not to consider me to be a treacherous
friend and an egotist for keeping it from you and de-
ceiving you. You see, I did it because I did not have
the strength to part from you and because I loved you
as my guardian angel. I am now zealously doing my
work and carrying out my duties as well as possible.
Eustaphy Ivanovich never uttered a word when I
walked past him yesterday. I cannot conceal from you,
dear heart, that I am greatly distressed about my debts
and the terrible condition of my wardrobe, but, again,
that does not matter very much, and I implore you, my
dear, not to be discouraged about it. You have sent me
another half rouble, and this half rouble cut me to the
quick. So that's how things are now, so that's how it
is, I mean that it is not I, the old fool, who am keeping
you, but you, poor little orphan-child, who are helping
me. Theodora has done well to have got that money.
For the time being, dear heart, I have no hope of getting more money, but if there is the slightest hope of
my getting any, I shall write to you about it all in
detail. It is gossip, gossip that worries me most of all.
Good-bye, my angel. I kiss your hand and beg you to
get better. I am not writing in more detail to you because I am in a hurry to go to the office, for it is by my
diligence and zeal that I can make good all my faults
and omissions in the service. I postpone the account of
my adventures and the affair with the army officers
until tonight.

Yours respectfully and sincerely loving,

Makar Devushkin.

July 28th.

Dear, oh dear! It is you, darling Barbara, who are wrong and, I'm sure, you'll regret it. You have completely puzzled and confounded me by your last letter and it is only now when at my leisure I have uncovered the most secret places of my heart that I realise I was right, absolutely right. I am not referring to my debauch (let's forget it, dear heart, let's forget it!) but to the fact that I love you and that it was not at all imprudent for me to love you, not at all. You know nothing, dear heart; if only you knew why I have to love you, why that is so, you wouldn't have said that. You only appear to be speaking sense, but I'm sure that deep down in your heart you do not believe it.

My darling, I don't know myself what happened last night between the army officers and myself. I think I ought to tell you, my angel, that up to that moment I was in a terrible state of confusion. For a whole month, you see, I was hanging by a thread. My position was most disastrous. I concealed it from you and from the people at home, but my landlady raised a terrible clamour. It wouldn't have mattered to me—let the silly woman scream as much as she likes—but for one thing, I couldn't help being ashamed, and for another, she found out—goodness only knows how—about our relationship and kept shouting about it all over the house so that I was stunned and stopped up my ears. But, unfortunately, the other people did not stop up their ears, but, on the contrary, took everything in. So now, dear heart, I simply don't know what to do.

It is all this, my angel, all this accumulation of all

sorts of disasters that finally finished me. Suddenly I
heard most extraordinary things from Theodora. It
seems an unworthy suitor had been to see you and had
insulted you with an improper proposal, that he had
offended you, deeply offended you. I say that because
that's exactly how I feel, dear heart, for I was deeply
offended myself. It was then, my angel, that I took
leave of my senses, it was then that I lost all self-
control and was done for. I rushed out, my dear
friend, in a state of terrible frenzy. I was going to call
on him, on that wicked blackguard. I did not know
what I wanted to do next, for I did not want you, my
angel, to be offended. Anyway, I felt terribly sick at
heart. The weather, too, was awful: rain, slush, terrible! I was about to return home. It was at that point,
dear heart, that I was undone. You see, I met Yemelyan Ilyich. He's a civil servant, I mean, he *was* a civil
servant but is no longer one because he has been
sacked. I don't know what he is doing now, how he
manages to make a living. So he and I went off together. Then—but, dear Barbara, I don't think you'd
enjoy reading about the misfortunes of your friend,
about his calamities and the temptations he has under-
gone. It was in the evening of the third day that
Yemelyan dared me to go to see that army officer, and
I went. I found out his address from the porter of our
house. As a matter of fact, dear heart, I had observed
that fellow a long time ago, I had kept an eye on him
when he lived in our house. Now, of course, I realise
that what I did was highly improper, but I was beside
myself when I was told about him. I really don't remember what happened exactly, Barbara. All I remember is that there were lots of army officers at his place

or, perhaps, I saw everything double—goodness only knows! Neither can I remember what I said, except that in my wild resentment I said many things. Well, it was then that they kicked me out, threw me down the stairs, not really threw me down, but just pushed me down. You know how I returned home—that's all. Of course, I made an ass of myself, and my pride has suffered a blow, but then no one knows about it, no one but you, that is, and in that case it's as if it never happened. Perhaps it didn't. What do you think, my dear? All I know for certain is that one of my colleagues, Aksenty Osipovich, did the same thing to Peter Petrovich, but it was all done in secret. Aksenty Osipovich called him into the duty room (I happened to see it all through a chink in the wall) and dealt with him in a way he deserved, but it was all done in a gentlemanly way, for no one except me saw it. Well, but I, you see, have nothing to fear. I mean to say, I told no one about it. After the scene between Aksenty Osipovich and Peter Petrovich nothing happened either. For, you see, Peter Petrovich is an ambitious man and he never told anyone about it, so that now they bow and shake hands. Mind you, Barbara, I'm not disposed to argue about it. I do not want to argue with you, I have suffered a terrible blow to my reputation, and what is even more awful, I have suffered a great deal in my own estimation, but I'm afraid it's just Fate—it must have been preordained that it should happen to me, and you can't escape your fate, as you well know. That, then, is a detailed account of my misfortunes and calamities—something you might as well not have read at all. I'm afraid I'm not feeling too well, dear heart, and am not quite my old playful self.

I should, therefore, like to confess to you my devotion, love, and respect and, my dear Miss Dobroselov, remain

> Your obedient servant,
> *Makar Devushkin.*

July 30th.

Dear Mr. Devushkin,

I have read your two letters and I did not know what to think of it all! Listen, my friend, you are either concealing something from me or you write only a part of all your troubles or. . . . Honestly, your letters still bear traces of some kind of confusion. Come and see me, for goodness' sake, come and see me today, and, please, come direct from the office and have dinner with us. I really don't know how you are living now and how you have come to terms with your landlady. You didn't write to me about that, and it seems as though you omitted to say anything about it on purpose. So good-bye, my friend, and don't forget to come and see me today. It would be much better if you dined here *always*. Theodora is an excellent cook. Good-bye.

> Yours,
> *Barbara Dobroselov.*

August 1st.

My dear Barbara,

You must be glad, my dear, that God has given you an opportunity for repaying good for good and that you can return my kindness. I believe it, dear Barbara, and I believe in the goodness of your angelic heart, and I'm not saying this to reproach you. Only, please do not scold me as you did when in my old age I spent more than I could afford. Well, that can't be helped, can it? I'm to blame, if, that is, you insist that I am. Only it does hurt me very much to hear you say so. I feel terrible about it myself. Poor people are capricious—it's a law of nature. I have felt it before, too. The poor man is exacting: he looks at everything in a different way, he looks round suspiciously at every passer-by and pricks up his ears at every word that is uttered: aren't those people talking about him? Are they commenting on his homely appearance? Aren't they doing that on purpose to make him feel uncomfortable? Does he look funny on that side or on the other? For everyone knows, my dear, that a poor man is worse than an old rag and cannot expect any respect from anyone, whatever those scribblers write— whatever they write about him—the poor man will remain as before. Why so? Because, according to them a poor man must not keep anything to himself, there must be nothing secret about him, he must have no self-respect—none! Yemelyan told me the other day that he had to undergo a means test, that he had to account to the authorities for every penny he earned. They suspected that they were doling out money for nothing—but no! they paid for the pleasure of beholding a poor man. Today, dear heart, even charity is dispensed in a strange way. But then, perhaps, it has always been like that—who knows? Either they don't know how to dispense it or they are real experts at it— one or the other. You probably did not know that— well, you know it now! We may be wrong about anything else, but not about this! Why does the poor man know all this? Why is he aware of it? Why? Well, from experience! He knows, for instance, that quite near there is a certain gentleman who, when he enters a restaurant, says to himself, I wonder what that ragged civil servant will be eating today? I'll be eating some *cotellettes en papillotes*, while he'd be lucky to eat anything more than buckwheat porridge without butter! And what business is it of his if I do eat buckwheat porridge without butter? There are such people, my dear, there are people who think like that. And it is they, the disgusting muckrakers, who keep looking at you whether you step on a stone with the whole of your foot or only with your toe, whether some low-grade civil servant of a certain department has got his bare toes protruding from his boot or his elbows from his torn sleeves, and then they write it all up and publish such rubbish. What business is it of theirs whether my elbows protrude or not? If you will forgive, my dear Barbara, what may seem to you a rude remark, the poor man's sense of shame can be compared in this respect to your maidenly modesty. For you would not—forgive my indiscretion—undress before everybody, would you? In the same way does a poor man object to people peering into his hovel to see what his family relationships are like. Yes, indeed! What they do is to offend me by treating me in the same way as my enemies who try to deprive an honest man of his honour and self-respect!

At the office, too, today I sat like a bear-cub, like a plucked sparrow, so that I fairly burned with shame. Yes, my dear Barbara, I was terribly ashamed. Indeed, it is only natural to be ashamed when your bare elbows show through the holes of your coat and your buttons are hanging by a single thread. As though on

purpose, everything about me was in such disorder.
Why, Stepan Karlovich himself started talking about
some office business to me today, he talked and talked
and then, as though casually, added: "Dear me, Mr.
Devushkin . . . " but did not finish what he wanted to
say. But I, of course, guessed what he had in mind and
blushed all over so that even the bald patch on my
head turned red. Not that it matters, but it makes you
feel uncomfortable and gives rise to painful thoughts.
Have they found out something? Good Lord, what if
they had found out! To tell the truth, I greatly suspect
one individual. Those villains don't care a damn!
They'd betray you! Betray your private life for a farthing! They hold nothing sacred, they don't!

I know now who it is—it's Ratazyaev. He knows
someone in our department, and I'm sure has told him
all about me with all sorts of trimmings. Or he might
have spoken about me in his department and the story
has spread to our department. For at home everyone
knows everything, down to the last detail, and they
each point a finger at your window. I know they do
that. Yesterday, when I went across to have dinner
with you, they all thrust their heads out of their
windows, and my landlady said that the old devil
seemed to be cradle-snatching and then she called
you a bad name. But all that is nothing compared with
Ratazyaev's odious plan to put you and me in one of
his stories and describe us in some clever satire. He
had said so himself, and I was told about it by some
of our more decent lodgers. I simply don't know what
to think about it, dear heart, and can't make up my
mind what to do. We must have angered the Lord,
you and I, my angel. You were going to send me some

book, dear heart, to keep my mind off my troubles. I'd rather you did not send it. What's the use of a book? It's just a piece of fiction! A novel, too, is nonsense and written as such for idle people to read. Believe me, dear heart. Trust my long experience. And what if they do try to change your mind by mentioning Shakespeare to you, that, you see, there's a Shakespeare in literature—well, Shakespeare, too, is nonsense, all this is a lot of nonsense and is written solely for the sake of lampooning people!

Your
Makar Devushkin.

August 2nd.

Dear Mr. Devushkin,

Don't worry about anything. God willing, everything will be all right. Theodora got lots of work for herself and me, and we have set about it with a will. Perhaps it will all come right in the end. Theodora suspects that all my recent troubles are not unknown to Anna Fyodorovna, but I don't care any more. Somehow, I feel extraordinarily cheerful today. You are thinking of borrowing money—the Lord preserve you from such a step. You will be in real trouble afterwards when the time comes to repay your debts. You'd better come and see us more often and spend more time with us. Don't pay any attention to your landlady. As for your other enemies and ill-wishers, I'm sure you are worrying about nothing. Pay more attention to your style—I believe I told you it is extremely uneven. Well, good-bye, *au revoir.* Don't forget to come and see me!

Yours,
B.D.

August 3rd.

My angel Barbara,

I hasten to inform you, dear life, that my hopes are rising again. But, really, my darling little daughter, you say that I mustn't incur any more debts. But, my sweet child, one can't carry on without them. I'm not too well and what if you, too, were to fall ill suddenly? You're not too strong, are you? That's why I'm writing to you that I simply have to borrow some money. Well, to continue.

I must tell you, Barbara, that at the office I sit next to Yemelyan Ivanovich. He is not the Yemelyan you know. He, like myself, is a civil servant of the lowest grade, and he and I are almost the oldest and most indigenous officials in our department. He's a good man, a disinterested soul, taciturn and rather surly looking. But, on the other hand, he is efficient, has an excellent English hand, indeed, if truth be told, his handwriting is just as good as mine—a very worthy man. We have never been on intimate terms with each other, just hail-fellow-well-met—good morning, good-bye. If I had to borrow a penknife occasionally, I would ask him: please may I have your penknife, Yemelyan Ivanovich. In short, the ordinary civilities demanded by convention. Well, so he said to me this morning: Makar Alexeyevich, what's worrying you? I could see that he wished me well, so I told him everything—no, not everything, God forbid—for I could never do that, I wouldn't have the courage, but I did tell him a few things, that I'm in financial difficulties and so on. "But why don't you borrow a little money?" said Yemelyan Ivanovich. "You can borrow some from Peter Petrovich, he lends money on interest. I borrowed some money from him myself. He charges fair rates of interest—not too burdensome!" Well, Barbara, I confess my heart missed a beat. I kept thinking that perhaps the Good Lord would put into the mind of Peter Petrovich to let me have a loan. I was already making plans to pay my landlady, help you, and get myself some decent clothes, for my clothes are a disgrace: I feel ashamed to sit down in them, not to mention the fact that our clever fellows keep scoffing and laughing at me—not that it matters to me! Besides, the head of our department sometimes passes through our section and he might—God forbid!—glance at me and notice how disgracefully I am dressed. And he is a great stickler for neatness and cleanliness. Not that he would say anything, but I'd die of shame—yes, indeed! In consequence of it all, plucking up courage and hiding my shame in my empty pocket, I went to see Peter Petrovich, full of hope and more dead than alive from my expectations—and from one thing and another. Well, my dear Barbara, the whole thing came to nothing. He seemed to be busy. He was talking to Fedosey Ivanovich. I sidled up to him, pulled him by the elbow, and called him by his name. He looked round, and I told him about the plight I was in and that I wanted to borrow thirty roubles, and so on. At first he did not seem to grasp what I wanted, but when I had explained everything to him, he just laughed and, well, did not say anything. I repeated my request, and he said: "Have you any security?" He then buried himself in his papers and went on writing without looking at me. I must say I was a little taken aback. "No, sir," I said to him, "I have no security," and I went on to explain that as soon as I got my salary, I would pay him back, that he could count on me to do so, that I'd consider it to be my duty. At that moment someone called him away. I waited; he came back and began to sharpen his pen, as though he did not notice I was there. But I went on repeating: "Don't you think, Peter Petrovich, you could arrange it somehow?" He did not utter a word, just as though he did not hear anything. I stood there for a little while longer, then I thought, "Let's try for the last time," and I pulled at his sleeve. He never said a word, sharpened his quill pen and started writing. So I went away. You see, dear heart, they may be excellent fellows all of them, but they are proud, very proud—not like me! We can never hope to vie with them, Barbara. That's why I told you all that. Yemelyan Ivanovich also laughed and shook his head, but he did hold out some hope to me, the good fellow. Yemelyan Ivanovich is a worthy man. He has promised to introduce me to a certain man he knows who lives in the Vyborsky suburb and who also lends money on interest. A low-grade civil servant. Yemelyan Ivanovich is sure he will let me have some money. I'm going to call on him tomorrow. What do you think about it, my angel? I simply have to borrow some money! My landlady threatens to turn me out of my room and refuses to serve me dinners. My boots, too, are boots in need of repair, dear heart, and the buttons of my coat are all gone—and that's not all, by any means! What if my superiors should notice such impropriety? It's dreadful, my dear, dreadful, simply dreadful!

Makar Devushkin.

August 4th.

Dear Mr. Devushkin,

For god's sake, Mr. Devushkin, try to borrow some money as soon as possible. I wouldn't ask you for help in your present circumstances, but if only you knew what my situation was like now. We cannot remain in our present lodgings any longer. Something awful has happened, and you cannot imagine how upset and agitated I am. Just think, my friend: this morning, an elderly, almost old man called on us. I was surprised, for I had no idea what he wanted. Theodora had gone out shopping just then. He began questioning me about the sort of life I lead and what sort of work I do and, without waiting for an answer, informed me that he was the uncle of the officer you told me about. He said that he was very angry with his nephew for the way he had behaved and for having spread scandalous stories about me all over town, that his nephew was a guttersnipe and a fellow of no decent principles and that he was ready to take me under his protection; he advised me to have nothing to do with young men, adding that he sympathised with me just as if he were my own father, that he entertained fatherly feelings towards me and would be glad to help me in any way he could. I kept blushing, for I did not know what to make of it all, but I was not in a hurry to thank him. Then he took me forcibly by the hand, patted my cheek, said that I was a very pretty girl and that he was extremely pleased that I had dimples in my cheeks (goodness knows what else he said) and at last he tried to kiss me, saying that he was sure I wouldn't mind because he was an old man (he was such a nasty man!). At that moment Theodora returned. He looked a little embarrassed and said that he respected me for my modesty and my good behaviour and that he hoped I would get better acquainted with him. Then he took Theodora aside and tried under some strange pretext to give her some money, which she, of course, declined to take. At last he went, after once more repeating his assurances and saying that he intended to pay me another visit and that he would bring me some earrings (he seemed rather embarrassed), that he advised me to change my lodgings and recommended me a beautiful apartment which he knew of and which would cost me nothing. Finally, he declared that he liked me very much for being an honest and sensible girl, advised me to beware of dissolute young men, and concluded by saying that he knew Anna Fyodorovna and that Anna Fyodorovna had asked him to tell me that she would shortly visit me herself. I understood everything then. I was beside myself. For the first time in my life I had found myself in such a situation. I was furious and made the old man thoroughly ashamed of himself. Theodora helped me and practically threw him out of our flat. We decided that it must all be the work of Anna Fyodorovna, for how would he otherwise have got to know about us?

Now I'm turning to you, Mr. Devushkin, and beg you to help me. Do not, for God's sake, leave me in the lurch. Please, borrow some money, get all the money you can, for we can't afford to move to other lodgings and we can't possibly stay here any longer. Theodora is of the same opinion. We need at least twenty-five roubles; I'll pay you back; I'll earn the money. Theodora will get me some additional work soon, so that if they ask you to pay a big interest on the loan, don't hesitate but agree to pay. I'll repay everything, only for heaven's sake do not refuse to help me. You can't imagine what it costs me to trouble you now when you yourself are so hard up, but you are my only hope. Goodbye, Mr. Devushkin. Think of me, and may the Lord grant you success!

B.D.

August 4th.

My darling Barbara,

These unexpected blows have shaken me terribly. It is these awful calamities that have broken my spirit. Not only is this rabble of all sorts of toadies and disgusting old men trying to undermine your health, my angel, not only that—these lickspittles are trying to destroy me too. And they will destroy me, they will, I swear they will. You see, I'd rather die than refuse to help you. Indeed, if I do not help you, I shall die Barbara—I mean it literally, but were I to help you, you'd fly away out of the nest, like a bird, which these owls, these birds of prey, are trying to peck to death. It is this thought that is torture to me, dear heart. And you, Barbara, you, too, are so cruel! How could you have thought of it? You are harrassed, you are insulted, you, my sweet little bird, are suffering, and are grieved to have to trouble me and you promise to pay off your debt by obtaining more work, which means— to tell the truth—that you are prepared to ruin your weak constitution in order to repay my loan at the right time. Just think what you are saying, dear Barbara! Why should you sew, why should you work,

torture your poor head with anxiety, hurt your beautiful eyes and ruin your health? Why, dear Barbara,
don't you see, my darling? that I am no good at all?
But I'll do my best to be of some good to you. I will
overcome every difficulty, I'll get some extra work myself, I'll copy out all sorts of manuscripts for writers,
I'll go and see them myself, I'll make them give me
work. For, you see, dear heart, they are looking for
good copyists, I know they are, and I won't let you
overwork. I won't let you carry out your disastrous
plan. I shall raise a loan, my angel, I promise you. I'd
rather die than not do so. You write that I should not
be deterred by a high rate of interest, and I shall not,
dear heart, I shall not be deterred. Nothing will deter
me now. I shall ask for forty roubles, dear heart. It's
not much, is it? What do you think? Would anyone
trust me with forty roubles to begin with? What I
mean is, do you think I am capable of inspiring con-
fidence at first sight? I mean, would anyone get
a favourable impression of me from my face at the
first glance? Try to remember, my angel, am I capable
of giving such an impression? What do you think? You
know, I can't help feeling afraid—terribly, truly, terribly afraid. Out of the forty roubles, I'm going to set
aside twenty-five for you, dear Barbara, two for my
landlady and the rest for my own expenses. As a matter of fact, I ought to give more than two to my landlady—I must give her more, in fact. But when you
consider everything, dear heart, when you take account of all my needs, you will see that I can't possibly
give her more, so it's no use talking about it or mentioning it. For one rouble I shall buy myself a new pair

of boots. I really don't know whether I shall be able
to go to the office in my old boots tomorrow. I also
must get myself a new scarf, for the one I'm wearing
will soon have passed its first year. But as you have
promised to make me not only a scarf but also a shirt
front out of your old pinafore, I need not worry any
longer about a new scarf. So much for the boots and
scarf. Now for buttons. You will agree, my little one,
that I cannot do without buttons. Almost half the buttons on my coat are missing! I shudder to think what
the head of our department may say on noticing such
disorder. Say? Why, dear heart, I shan't hear what he
says, for I'll drop dead, I'll drop dead on the spot—
drop dead with shame, from the very thought of it. Indeed, dear heart! I shall be left with three roubles,
after having provided for all my necessities, which I
shall spend on food and half a pound of tobacco, for,
my angel, I cannot live without tobacco, and it's nine
days since I last put a pipe into my mouth. To tell the
truth, I should have bought the tobacco without telling you, but I'd be ashamed to do that. You're in
great trouble, you're depriving yourself of everything,
and I'd be indulging in all sorts of pleasures. That's
why I'm telling you all this, so as not to be tortured by
pricks of conscience. I tell you frankly, dear Barbara,
that I have never been in such straitened circumstances before. My landlady despises me, and no one
shows me any respect. I'm terribly hard up, I'm in
debt, and at the office where my colleagues have never
made my life particularly pleasant, they certainly don't
make it any more pleasant now. I hide, I carefully hide
everything from everybody, and every time I enter the

office I sidle in, shunning everyone. I have just enough presence of mind to confess this to you. But what if he refuses to lend me the money! Well, darling, better not think of it, better not let such thoughts discourage me completely. I am writing this to you to warn you not to think of it yourself, nor to torture yourself with such bitter thoughts. Dear Lord, what's to become of you then? It's true, of course, that in that case you won't leave your lodgings and I'll stay with you, but no! I shall not return then, I shall simply disappear, vanish without a trace. Dear me, I've been writing this long letter to you but I really should have been shaving—it makes a much better impression, and a good impression is always effective. Well, God grant that I shall be successful! I'll say a prayer and be off!

M. Devushkin

August 5th

Dearest Mr. Devushkin,

I wish you at least would not despair! There is plenty of trouble without that. I am sending you thirty copecks in silver. I'm sorry I cannot send more. Buy yourself what you most need so that you could at least keep going till tomorrow. We have almost nothing left, and I don't know what I am going to do tomorrow. It's a sad business! Still, don't worry too much. If you have not succeeded in raising the loan, it can't be helped, can it? Theodora says that it doesn't matter that we can stay in our lodgings for some time longer, that even if we left, we wouldn't have gained a lot, for if they wanted to, they could find us anywhere. Still I don't think somehow that it's a good thing for us to remain here. If I didn't feel so sad, I'd tell you something.

What a strange man you are, Mr. Devushkin! You take everything too much to heart. That's why you'll always be very unhappy. I read your letters very carefully and I can see that in each letter you worry about me as you never do about yourself. Everyone, of course, will say that you have a kind heart, but I say that it is a little too kind. Let me give you a piece of friendly advice, Mr. Devushkin. I am grateful, very grateful to you for all you have done for me—I do appreciate it very much. You can, therefore, imagine what I feel when I see that even now, after all the troubles of which I have been the involuntary cause, that even now you live for me alone—for my joys, for my sorrows, for my affection! If one takes so much to heart everything that happens to another person and if one sympathizes so strongly with her, then indeed one can make oneself the unhappiest man in the world. Today, when you came to see me after the office, you frightened me: you looked so pale, so scared, so desperate—you looked awful! And all because you were afraid to tell me of your failure to raise a loan, you were afraid to grieve and alarm me. When you saw that I nearly burst out laughing, you felt almost relieved. My dear Mr. Devushkin, do not be so dejected, do not despair, be more sensible, I beg of you, I implore you. You'll see everything will be all right, everything will change for the better. You will find life unbearable if you go on worrying about another person's troubles. Good-bye, my friend. I implore you not to worry too much about me.

B.D.

August 5th.

My darling Barbara,

Very well, my angel, very well! You have decided that it doesn't matter that I have not got the money. Very well, I'm relieved and happy on your account. Indeed, I am delighted that you are not deserting an old fellow like me and are not leaving your present lodgings. To be quite frank, my heart overflowed with joy when I read the nice things you wrote about me in your letter and rendered proper recognition to my sentiments. I say this not out of pride but because I realise how much you love me to be so worried about my kind heart. Very well, no need to mention my kind heart any more now. A kind heart is one thing, but you are also telling me, dear heart, not to be faint-hearted. Well, my angel, I quite agree that there is no need to be faint-hearted, but all the same could you tell me, dear heart, what boots I am going to wear at the office tomorrow! There's the rub, dear heart, I mean this kind of thought may very well cause the ruin of a man, his complete ruin. The main thing, my dear, is that I'm not suffering for myself or worrying about myself: it does not matter to me that I should have to walk in a hard frost without an overcoat and without boots. I can bear it, I can endure it all, for I am a small, simple man. But what will people say? What will my enemies, what will evil tongues be saying when I am seen walking without an overcoat? Besides, I expect one even wears boots for their sake. In that case, dear heart, dearest darling, I need a pair of boots for the sake of my reputation and my good name. Boots with holes would spell ruin to both—trust, dear heart, my long experience, listen to an old man who knows both the world and people, and not some stupid scribblers.

But I have not yet told you in detail, dear heart, what happened today, what I had to endure today. What I had to go through, the agony of mind I had to suffer in one morning which another man would not have suffered in one year. This is what happened: first of all I went out early in the morning to see the man I have mentioned and be in time for the office. It was raining cats and dogs, and the slush was indescribable! I wrapped myself in my winter cloak, my sweet darling, and I walked and walked, thinking all the time: "Lord forgive me my transgressions and send me fulfilment of my desires." I passed a church, I crossed myself and confessed all my sins. Then it occurred to me that it was unworthy of me to strike a bargain with God. I became so absorbed in myself that I did not look at anything and walked on without looking where I was going. The streets were deserted, and if I did meet anyone, he, too, was worried and preoccupied, and no wonder, for who would choose to go out so early and in such weather! I met a crowd of grimy workmen on the way and was jostled by them. The peasants! I was overcome by panic, I felt nervous, and, frankly, I was unwilling even to think of the money—but why not take a chance? Near the Voskresensky Bridge one of my soles fell off and I did not know what I was walking on. Next I met Yemelyan, a clerk in our office. He drew himself up to his full height, stood still and followed me with his eyes as though asking me for a tip: dear me, I thought to myself, a tip indeed! What kind of a tip can you expect from me, my dear fellow? I was terribly tired, I stopped for a moment, had a little rest, and dragged myself along further. I kept staring at things on purpose for something to attach my thoughts to, to distract myself, to pluck up courage, but no! I could not attach my thoughts to anything; besides, I had got so bedraggled that I felt ashamed of myself. At last I saw from a distance a yellow-timbered house with an attic in the form of a belvedere. Well, I said to myself, that must be it—so Yemelyan Ivanovich had told me—that must be Markov's house. (It's Markov, dear heart, who lends money on interest.) Hardly conscious of what I was doing, for I knew very well that it was Markov's house, I asked a policeman whose house it was. The policeman, a coarse fellow, answered reluctantly, as though he were cross with someone, speaking without opening his mouth, that it was indeed Markov's house. Policemen are all such unfeeling brutes—but it was not only the policeman! Everything made a bad and unpleasant impression on me: everything, in short, seemed to point to one and the same thing, everything seemed to reflect my own situation, and it's always like that. I walked three times past the house and along the street, and the longer I walked, the worse I felt—No! I thought to myself, he won't give me any money, not for anything in the world! He does not know me, and my business is rather precarious, nor is my figure exactly impressive. Oh well, I thought, what will be, will be, so long as I shan't be sorry afterwards, they won't murder me for trying! I opened the gate quietly, but as ill luck will have it, a stupid, wretched watch-dog rushed upon me, barking fit to burst itself! It is such disgusting trivial incidents, dear heart, that infuriate a man and make him frightened and destroy the determination he has armed himself with. So I entered the house more dead than alive, walked straight in, unfortunately, for in the dark I failed to notice something on the floor near the threshold and, slipping, stumbled against some peasant woman who was filling a milk jug from a pail and who spilled all the milk. The silly creature screamed and raised an awful din. "Look where you're going, you old devil!" she shouted. "What do you want?" And she went on abusing me at the top of her voice. I'm telling you this, dear heart, because this sort of thing always happens to me in such circumstances. It seems to me to have been ordained like that; I invariably knock against something. The mistress of the house, an old beldame, a Finnish woman, ran out to see what the noise was about, and I addressed myself straight to her: "Does Mr. Markov live here?" "No, sir," she replied, but after standing still and examining me closely, she asked: "What do you want him for?" I told her about Yemelyan Ivanovich and explained that I had come on business. The old woman called her daughter—a barefoot girl who was getting on in years —and told her to summon her father, who was upstairs talking to their lodgers. She showed me into their drawing-room, quite a nice room, portraits on the walls, all of them of generals, a sofa, a round table, pots of mignonettes and balsam. I kept wondering whether I should not clear out while there was still time, and to tell you the truth, dear heart, I wanted to run away. I could come again tomorrow, I thought, the weather might be better, or I could wait a day or two more. Just now I had spilled the milk, and the generals, too, were looking at me so angrily. I made for the door, but at that moment Mr. Markov came in: nothing special, grey hair, a pair of thievish little eyes, in a dirty dressing gown fastened with a cord. He asked me what my business was and I told him— Yemelyan Ivanovich—forty roubles—and so on, but I never finished, for I could see from the look in his eyes that it was no use. "Well," he said, "I see your point, but I'm sorry I have no money. You haven't got any security, have you?" I tried to explain that I had no security, but that Yemelyan Ivanovich—I told him everything, in short. He heard me out, then said: "I'm afraid Yemelyan Ivanovich is wrong: I have no money!" Well, I thought, so that's that, I knew it, I foresaw it. I mean, Barbara, that it would have been much better if the earth had opened up under my feet. I felt so cold, my legs went numb, a cold shiver ran down my back. I looked at him, and he looked at me as if to say, "Well, my dear fellow, you'd better go. There's nothing more for you to do here!" Anywhere else I should have sunk into the ground for shame. "What do you want that money for?" (That's what he actually asked me, dear heart!) I was about to open my mouth, but he would not listen to me. "No, sir," he said, "I have no money. Why, it would have been a pleasure . . ." I kept repeating that it was not a lot of money, that I'd repay him, repay him in time, ahead of time, that he might charge me what interest he liked, and that I would repay him—really and truly! You see, dear heart, at that moment I remembered all your troubles and all your needs, I remembered the half rouble you had given me. "No, sir," he said. "Why talk of interest? Now if you had some security . . . You see, I have no money, otherwise I should have lent you some, I swear by God, I should!" Sworn by God, the brigand!

Well, my dear, I simply don't remember how I left the house, how I walked through the Vyborsky suburb, how I found myself on Voskresensky Bridge. I was terribly tired, chilled to the bone, shivering with cold, and I only managed to get to the office at ten o'clock. I tried to clean myself up, get the mud off my clothes, but Snegiyov, our porter, said that I couldn't do that, because, he said, I might spoil the brush, and "The brush, sir," he said, "is government property." So that's how they are treating me now, dear heart. These gentlemen regard me as worse than a rag you wipe your feet on. For you see, Barbara, what hurts me is not lack of money, but all these trivial worries of everyday life, all those whisperings, those smiles, those little jokes. His Excellency, the head of our department, might somehow chance to put it all down to me. Ah, my dear, my golden days are gone!

Today I reread all your letters: it is sad, dear heart. Good-bye, my dear, the Lord guard you!

Makar Devushkin.

P. S. I'd have liked to have described my misfortunes today in a half-humorous vein, but it seems humour is not my forte. I wanted to please you. I'll come and see you, dear heart, I'll come for certain, I'll come tomorrow.

August 11th.

Dear Barbara, my darling, dear heart, I am undone, both of us are undone, irretrievably undone. My reputation, my self-respect—everything is lost. I'm done for and you are done for, dear heart, you as well as I are done for irretrievably. It was I, I who have been your ruination. I'm persecuted, dear heart, I'm despised and laughed at, and my landlady has simply begun abusing me. She shouted and shouted at me today, scolded and scolded me, and treated me worse than dirt. Last night at Ratazyaev's, one of the fellows began reading the draft of a letter which I had written to you and which I had inadvertently pulled out of my pocket. My dear, how they jeered at me! They called us all sorts of names, the traitors, and they kept laughing at the top of their voices! I walked in and accused Ratazyaev of treachery. I told him he was a traitor. But Ratazyaev said that I was a traitor myself, that I was occupied with all sorts of conquests. "You have kept it a secret from us," he said. "You are a Lovelace." Now they all call me Lovelace. I am not known by any other name. You see, my angel, you see, they know everything now, they have found everything out, they know all about you, too, my dear, all about your affairs, they know everything! Why, Faldoni is in league with them. Today I told him to go to the sausage shop for something, but he just refused to go. "I'm busy," he said. "But it's your duty to go," I said. "Not at all," he replied, "it is not my duty. You don't pay your rent to my mistress, so it's not my duty to run your errands for you!" I could not tolerate such an insult from an ignorant peasant and I called him a fool. He said, "You're a fool yourself." I thought that he was so rude to me because he had been drinking, so I said to him: "You're drunk, you stupid oaf!" To which he replied: "You haven't offered me any drink, have you? Why, you haven't any money to buy a drink for yourself. You've been cadging for a few copecks from a certain young lady, haven't you?" And he added: "Calls himself a gentleman, too!" So you see, my dear, how far it's gone! I'm ashamed to be alive, Barbara. I feel like one possessed! Worse than a vagrant. What terrible misfortunes! I'm done for, simply done for, irretrievably done for!

                                        Makar Devushkin.

                                        August 13th.

Dearest Mr. Devushkin,

We seem to have nothing but misfortunes, and I don't know myself what to do. What's going to happen to you now, for I'm afraid there's little hope of my being able to help you: I burned my left hand on the iron today. I dropped it accidentally, bruised myself and burned myself at the same time. I can't do any work, and Theodora has not been well for the last three days. I'm in a state of agonising anxiety. I send you thirty copecks in silver. It's really all we possess, and, God knows, I wish I could help you now when you're in such great need. I could weep with vexation! Good-bye, my friend. I'd be so grateful to you if you'd come and see me today.

                                        B.D.

                                        August 14th.

Dear Mr. Devushkin,

What is the matter with you? You have no fear of God, I'm sure of it. You are simply driving me mad. Aren't you ashamed of yourself? You're ruining yourself. Just think of your reputation! You're an honest, honourable, self-respecting man—well what if people find out how you are behaving? Why, you should die

of shame! Have you no consideration for your grey
hairs? Have you no fear of God? Theodora has told
me that she would not do anything for you now, and
I'm not going to give you any more money, either.
Look what you have driven me to, dear Mr. Devushkin. Do you think that it's nothing to me that you are
behaving so badly? You don't seem to realise what I
have to put up with on your account. I cannot put a
foot on our stairs: everyone stares at me, points a
finger at me and says all sorts of horrible things about
me. Why, they even say I have got myself involved
with a drunkard. You don't think I like to hear that,
do you? When you are brought home drunk, all our
lodgers point at you with contempt. Look, they say,
they've just brought *that* civil servant back. I'm terribly ashamed for you. I swear I'm going to leave this
place. I'll get a job as a parlour-maid or a laundress.
I'm not going to stay here. I wrote to you to come and
see me, but you have not come. So, I suppose, my
tears and entreaties are nothing to you. And where
did you get the money? For heaven's sake, be more
careful. You'll be done for, you'll ruin yourself for
nothing. Think of the shame and disgrace! Your landlady would not even let you in last night. You spent
the night in the passage. I know it all. If only you
knew how upset I was when I heard about it. Come
and see us, Mr. Devushkin, you'll feel more cheerful
here: we will read together, we'll talk of old times,
Theodora will tell us of her pilgrimages to the holy
shrines. For my sake, my darling, don't ruin yourself
and don't ruin me. I live for you alone, and I am still
here with you for your sake. So that's how you are

now! Be an honourable man, resolute in the face of misfortunes. Remember that poverty is no crime. Anyway, why despair? It's all temporary. God willing, everything will come right. Only you must hold out now. I am sending you twenty copecks. Buy some tobacco or anything else you like, only for goodness' sake don't spend it on something bad. Come and see us, be sure to come. You may perhaps feel ashamed as before, but don't be ashamed—it's false shame. Only bring sincere repentance with you. Put your trust in God. He will put everything right.

B.D.

August 19th.

Dear heart,

I feel ashamed, my darling Barbara, I feel terribly ashamed! However, what's the fuss about, dear heart? Why not try to cheer up? I'm not thinking of the soles of my boots, then, for a sole is just rubbish and will always remain an ordinary, disgusting, filthy sole. Boots, too, are just rubbish. The Greek philosophers used to walk about without boots, so why should the likes of us make a fuss over such unworthy things? Why, then, should I be insulted and despised in that case? Oh, dear heart, dear heart, the things you thought it necessary to write to me! Tell Theodora that she's a crazy, loud-voiced, violent *and* stupid, unutterably stupid woman. As for my grey hairs, I'm afraid you're quite mistaken, my dear, for I'm not as old as you think. Yemelyan sends you his regards. You write that you are greatly upset and have been crying. In conclusion, let me wish you the best of health and happiness. As for me, I, too, am in good health and happy and remain, my angel,

Your friend,
Makar Devushkin.

August 21st.

My dear friend, Miss Dobroselov,

I feel that I am to blame, that I have wronged you and, in my opinion, dear heart, nothing is to be gained from the fact that I feel this way, whatever you may say. Even before I had done that thing, I felt as I do now, but I lost heart even while I was conscious of doing wrong. Dear heart, I am neither wicked nor cruel; to rend your little soul, my darling, one would have to be a bloodthirsty tiger, while I have the heart of a sheep and, as you well know, I have no inclination for bloodthirstiness. Therefore, my darling, I am not to be blamed for what I have done, neither are my heart nor my thoughts to be blamed. In fact, I don't know whose fault it is. I'm afraid, dear heart, the whole thing is a mystery. You sent me thirty and then twenty copecks; I felt sick at heart as I looked at your money, the money of a poor orphan. You burned your hand, and I expect you will be starving soon, and yet you write to me to buy myself some tobacco. What was I to do in that case? Go on robbing you, an orphan, like a brigand without any feeling or comprehension? It was at that point, dear heart, that I took courage. That is to say, feeling that I am no good and that I am no better than the sole of my boot, I decided that it was unseemly to regard myself as of any conse-quence, and indeed began to look upon myself as un-seemly and, to some extent, indecent. Well, the

moment I lost my self-respect and denied the existence
of my own good qualities and my own dignity, I decided to let everything go by the board—and that was
my downfall! It had been decreed by fate, and I cannot be held responsible for it. At first, I went out for
a breath of fresh air. Then one thing followed another: the weather was cold, and nature, too, was so
tearful. It was raining and, well, Yemelyan happened
to pass by. He had pawned everything he possessed,
Barbara, everything had been squandered, and at the
time I met him he hadn't had a bite for two whole
days. He had tried to pawn things no pawnbroker
would look at, for they were worthless as pledges. So,
you see, my dear, I gave in more out of pity for humanity than out of my inability to resist temptation.
That's how it all happened, dear heart. We talked of
you. We shed tears together. He is a most kind man.
Yes, indeed, a very kind man, a man who feels deeply.
I, too, dear heart, feel everything deeply; it's because I
am so sensitive that all these things happen to me. I
am aware, darling, how greatly I am indebted to you.
Having got to know you, I began to know myself better and to love you. Before I met you, I had been a
lonely man and had seemed to be asleep. I had not
lived at all. They—those villains I lodge with—used to
say that I cut so sorry a figure that they were loath to
be seen with me, and, well, I began to feel disgusted
with myself; they used to say that I was stupid, and I
began to think that I really was stupid. But when you
appeared, you shed so bright a light on my dark life
that my heart and soul were flooded with light, and I
found peace of mind and realised that I was no worse
than other men and that while I do not possess bril-

liance or polish or aristocratic manners, I am a man
for all that, a man in heart and mind. But at that moment I felt that I was persecuted by Fate, that, humiliated by it, I was no longer conscious of my own
dignity and, dispirited by my misfortunes, I lost heart.
Since you know everything now, dear heart, I beseech
you humbly not to inquire any more into this matter,
for my heart is breaking and I feel miserable and
depressed.

I remain, dear heart, respectfully yours,
Makar Devushkin.

September 3rd.

I did not finish my last letter, Mr. Devushkin, because I found it too difficult to write. There are moments when I feel glad to be alone, to be unhappy, to
grieve all alone without anyone to share my feelings,
and such moments are beginning to come upon me
more and more often. In my memories there is something I cannot explain, but that enthrals me so unac-
countably, so peacefully, that for hours I remain
insensible to anything around me and I forget everything, everything that is real. Indeed, there is not a
single impression in my present life—whether pleasant or painful or sad—which does not remind me of
something similar in my past, and most of all in my
childhood, my golden childhood. But after such moments I always feel unhappy. I seem to feel weak, my
reveries exhaust me, and my health—bad as it is—is
getting worse and worse.

But it is on such a fresh, sunny, brilliant morning—
as we seldom get in the autumn—that I feel invigor-
ated and I greet it joyfully. And so it's already autumn!

How I loved the autumn in the country! I was still a child, but even then I felt a great deal. And so it is autumn already! I loved an autumn evening more than an autumn morning. I remember there was a lake at the foot of a hill a short distance from our house. This lake—I seem to see it even now—is wide and bright and as clear as crystal. When the evening is quiet—the lake is calm; there is not a rustle in the trees along its banks, the water is still as glass. Fresh! Cold! The dew falls on the grass, lights shimmer in the peasants' cottages on the bank, the herd is driven back—and just then I used to slip quietly out of the house to gaze at my lake, and I used to gaze at it for hours sometimes. The fishermen have lit a campfire at the edge of the water, and its light could be seen far away reflected in the water. The sky is so cold, so blue, and its edges are covered with fiery red shafts and these shafts of light grow fainter and fainter; the moon rises; the air is so resonant—you can hear everything so clearly: the quick flutter of a frightened little bird, the sharp snap of a reed in the light breeze, the splash of a fish in the water—everything, everything could be heard. A white mist rises over the blue water, thin and transparent. The distant objects grow dark; everything seems swallowed up in the mist, but close by everything stands out in sharp relief just as though it were carved with a chisel—the boat; the banks; the islands; a barrel thrown away and forgotten at the edge of the water, rocking hardly perceptibly; a willow branch with yellow leaves entangled in the rushes; a belated gull rising in the air and diving into the cold water, then again rising and disappearing in the mist.

I kept gazing and listening—it was all so strange and wonderful. And yet I was still a child, a baby.

Oh, I loved the autumn, the late autumn, when the corn had been harvested and the work in the fields brought to an end, when of an evening the village girls were gathering to play and sing in some cottage, when everyone was waiting for the coming of winter. Then everything would grow much darker, the sky would become overcast, yellow leaves would be strewn like paths at the edge of the bared woods, and the pine forest would turn blue and then black, especially in the evening when a damp mist descended and the trees could be glimpsed through the mist, looking like giants, like hideous and terrible apparitions. Every time I happened to lag behind during a walk, every time I dropped behind the rest and found myself walking alone, I felt scared and began to quicken my steps. I used to tremble like a leaf for fear that some terrible creature might suddenly thrust its face from inside the hollow of a tree; meanwhile, a wind would suddenly rise and rush through the woods, blowing, roaring, and howling so piteously, tearing hundreds of leaves from the lifeless branches and whirling them about in the air. Behind them a big flock of birds would sweep across the sky with a wild, piercing cry, covering it completely as though with a black pall. I used to be terrified, and just at that very moment I would hear someone—some voice—whispering: "Run, child, run! Don't be late! Things will be awful here in a moment. Run, child, run!" My heart would be gripped with fear, and I'd run and run till I was breathless and panting. I would come running home out of breath, and at home everything would be gay

and noisy. We, the children, would be given some
work to do: shelling peas or seeding poppies. The
green logs crackled in the stove; our mother looked on
happily at our work; our old nanny, Ulyana, told us
stories about the old days or hair-raising fairy-tales
about sorcerers and dead men. We, the children, hud-
dled closer to each other, though there was a smile on
our lips. Then suddenly we would all fall silent. Hark!
A noise! Someone's knocking! Not at all! That was
Frolovna's spinning-wheel droning. Oh, the laughter
that this would cause! And then at night we were too
frightened to sleep; we would have such terrible
dreams. I used to wake up and I did not dare to move
and lay shuddering under the blanket till dawn. But
in the morning I would get up as fresh as a daisy. I'd
look out of the window: the entire field would be covered with hoar-frost; the thin, autumn hoar-frost hung
on the bare branches; the lake would be covered with
ice as thin as a sheet of paper; a white mist would be
rising over the lake; the gay birds would twitter noisily.
The sun shone from a cloudless sky and the bright
sunbeams were breaking up the thin ice like glass. It
was light, bright, gay! The fire crackled in the stove
once more; we all sat down at the samovar; and our
black dog Polkan, chilled to the marrow during the
night, looked through the window, wagging his tail in
friendly fashion. A peasant rode past the windows on
a lively horse on his way to the woods for firewood.
Everyone was so happy, so cheerful! Oh, what a lovely
time my childhood was!

So now, carried away by my memories, I weep like
a child. I remember everything so clearly, so clearly,
all my past comes back to me so vividly, while the

present is so dim and so dark. What will be the end of it? What will be the end of it all? You know, I somehow can't help being convinced, being certain that I am going to die next autumn. I am very, very ill. I often think that I am going to die, but I should not like to die like this—to be laid to rest here. Perhaps I shall have to take to my bed again as I did last spring, for I have never really had time to recover. I feel very miserable now. Theodora has gone out for the day, and I am alone. I have for some time felt afraid to be left alone. I have a strange feeling that there is someone else in the room, that someone is speaking to me. This happens especially when I am thinking of something and suddenly recover from my reverie. It is then that I feel terribly frightened. That's why I have written this letter to you, for when I am writing, this feeling passes away. Good-bye. I must close for I have neither any more paper nor any time. I have only one rouble left from the money I saved up for my dress and my hat. You gave your landlady ten roubles. That's good. That will keep her quiet for a while.

Do get your clothes repaired somehow. Good-bye. I am so tired. I can't think why I am growing so weak. The slightest effort tires me. If I do get some more work, how am I to do it? That's what worries me so much.

B.D.

September 5th.

My darling Barbara,

All sorts of things have happened to me today, my angel. To begin with, I've had a headache all day. To get over it, I went out for a breath of fresh air along

the Fontanka Canal. It was a dark, damp afternoon. At
six o'clock it was already getting dark—just as it is now.
It was not raining, but the mist was as good as real
rain. Clouds sailed across the sky in long, broad strips.
Crowds of people were walking along the embankment, people, too, whose frightful faces brought on a
feeling of depression: drunken peasants; snub-nosed
Finnish peasant women, bareheaded and wearing
boots; artisans; cabmen; some poor civil servant hurry-
ing along on some business; street urchins; a lock-
smith's apprentice in a striped smock, haggard and un-
healthy looking, whose face seemed to have been
soaked in lubricating oil, carrying a lock in his hand;
an old soldier over six feet tall, offering paper knives
and copper rings for sale—such was the public. It was
the customary hour apparently for just such a public.
A navigable canal—Fontanka! Such a large number of
boats that it made one wonder how they could all find
room in so narrow a fairway. On the bridges were
peasant women selling damp treacle cakes and rotten
apples, and they all looked damp and dirty. Fontanka
is not exactly an ideal spot for a stroll! Wet granite
under your feet; at either side of you tall, dingy, grimy
buildings; mist below your feet and mist above your
head. A dark and melancholy evening!

By the time I had turned into Gorokhavaya Street
night had fallen and the gas lamps were beginning to
be lit. I have not been in Gorokhavaya Street for a
long time—I just could not manage it. What a noisy
street! What splendid shops and stores! Everything
glitters and sparkles, fabrics, flowers under bellglasses,
all sorts of hats with ribbons, you would think it was
all displayed for show. But no! There actually are

people who buy those things and give them to their
wives. A rich street! There are lots of German bakers
who live in the street—must be well-to-do, all of them.
Hundreds of carriages drive along it every minute—
how does the roadway support them all? Such magnificent carriages, too, with windows like mirrors, up-
holstered in silk and velvet; noblemen's lackeys
wearing epaulets and swords. I glanced into all the carriages, ladies were sitting in all of them, all dressed up,
must have been princesses and countesses. I suppose
at that hour they were all driving to balls or assemblies.
It would be interesting to see a princess or any great
lady at close quarters; I have never seen them, except,
of course, when, as now, I happened to look into their
carriages. I thought of you just then. Oh, my darling,
every time I think of you now, my heart fails me. Why,
dear Barbara, are you so unfortunate? You are not
worse than other people, are you, my angel? You're
good, beautiful, intelligent—why, then, has such an evil
fate fallen to your lot? Why does it always happen
that a good man is left in a state of desolation while
others have happiness thrust upon them? I know, I
know, dear heart, that one ought not to think like
that, that it smacks of free-thinking, but in all frank-
ness, to be quite truthful, why does the raven, Fate,
croak out happiness to one person who is still in his
mother's womb, while another goes out into the world
from an orphanage? Why, it does happen that happiness often falls to the lot of Ivanushka the Fool. "You,
Ivanushka the Fool," says Fate, "ransack your grand-
father's moneybags, eat, drink, and be merry, while
you, poor clod, lick your lips in anticipation, for that's
all you're good for, my dear fellow!" It is wrong, dear

heart, it is very wrong to think like that, but you can't help having such sinful thoughts. You, my darling, should have been driving in such a carriage! You should have caught the fancy of some general, not a fellow like me. You should be wearing silver and golden dresses and not an old cotton dress. You should not be thin and sickly as you are now, but fresh, plump, and rosy-cheeked like a sugar doll. Then I'd be happy if only I could glance at you from the street through your brightly lit windows, even if I could only catch a glimpse of your shadow. The very thought that you, my sweet, were joyful and happy, would make me happy too. But what are things like now? Not only have evil people ruined you, but some rotter, some libertine comes along and insults you. Just because he wears a perfectly fitting frock-coat and looks at you through a gold-mounted lorgnette, the impudent rascal imagines that he can do nothing wrong, and that one has to listen indulgently to his indecent proposals. But, my dear fellows, are you sure you can get away with it? But why is that all? It is because one is an orphan, because one is unprotected, because one has no powerful friend who could give one the support which is one's due. What sort of man is he, what sort of people are they who think nothing of insulting an orphan? They are worthless wretches and not men at all, just worthless wretches; they are registered, but they do not actually exist—I'm sure of that. That's what they are like, these men! In my opinion, my dear, the organ-grinder whom I met in Gorokhavaya Street is more likely to inspire respect than they. Though he walks about the streets all day long, toiling incessantly in an effort to earn some pittance for his bare existence, he is his own master, he supports himself. He does not want any charity, he labours to give people pleasure, like a wound-up mechanical device. "I will give you pleasure," he says, "any way I can." True, he is a pauper, nothing but a pauper, but at least he is an honourable pauper: he is tired, he is chilled to the marrow, but he goes on working—working in his own way, but still working. There are many honest people, dear heart, who may be earning little considering the usefulness of their work, but they bow to no one, they ask no one for bread. I, too, am like that organ-grinder, I mean, not exactly like him, but I am like him in the honourable, gentlemanly sense inasmuch as, like him, I labour as far as possible, as far as it lies in my power. I can do no more—and you cannot condemn a man for refusing to do something he knows he cannot do.

The reason why I have mentioned the organ-grinder, dear heart, is that today something happened that made me doubly aware of my poverty. I stopped to look at the organ-grinder. I had been worried by all sorts of thoughts, so I stopped to distract myself. I was standing there with some cabmen, a maidservant and a little girl with a dirty face and dress. The organ-grinder took up a position in front of someone's windows. Next I caught sight of a little boy about ten who would have been pretty if he had not looked so haggard and ill. He was barefoot and seemed to be dressed only in a shirt. He was standing with his mouth open, listening to the music—just like any boy of his age. His eyes were fixed on the dancing dolls of the German organ-grinder, while his arms and legs went numb with cold. He was shivering and sucking the end of his sleeve. I noticed that he had a bit of paper in his hands. A man passed by and threw a small coin to the organ-grinder: the coin fell straight into the rimmed box which showed a Frenchman dancing with some ladies. The moment the little boy heard the rattle of the coin, he started, looked round timidly, and apparently thought that it was I who had thrown the coin to the organ-grinder. He ran up to me with his hands shaking and, holding out the paper to me, said in a trembling voice: "A note, sir!" I unfolded the paper, and, well, its message was pretty familiar: "Kind sir, I am a very sick mother of three starving children, please help me now, for when I die, I shall not forget you, my benefactor, in the next world for not having forgotten my little ones now." Well, there was nothing extraordinary about that; it was clear enough: it was happening every day. But what was I to give them? I was terribly sorry. The poor little boy was blue with cold, he was probably hungry, and he was not lying, he was certainly not lying. I know this sort of situation. But it is abominable that these bad mothers do not take care of their children and send them out half naked into the cold with begging letters. She is probably a stupid woman of weak character. Perhaps she has no one to do anything for her, so she sits there cross-legged and, for all I know, a very sick woman. Still, she ought to know where to look for assistance, but then she may be just a dishonest woman who sends out a weak and starving child on purpose to deceive the public, regardless of whether her child gets ill or not. And what could the poor boy learn from these begging letters? He would only grow embittered with walking, running about begging. Lots of people in the streets, but they have no time for him. Their hearts are turned to stone, their words are cruel: "Away with you! Clear off! None of your tricks!" This is what he hears from everyone, and the child's heart grows hardened, and the poor, frightened boy shivers in vain with the cold, just like some little fledgling that has fallen out of the nest. His hands and feet are freezing, he is gasping for breath. Before you know, he'll begin to cough and quite soon illness, like some unclean creeping thing, will worm its way into his chest and, behold, death is already hovering over him in some ill-smelling corner, without any nursing, without any help—there you have his whole life! That's what life is like, sometimes! Dear me, Barbara, it's terrible to hear someone begging, pass him by, give nothing and say, "The Lord will provide." Some kind of begging can be easily resisted (there are all sorts of begging, dear heart). You are used to the long, drawn-out, drawling, carefully prepared, routine sort of supplication of the professional beggar. It isn't very hard to refuse him, for he has been at the job a long time; he is used to it and he will get over it, for he knows how to get over it. But some kind of begging is out of the ordinary, crude, terrible—like that today when I took the boy's letter. There was a beggar standing near at a fence who did not ask anyone else that happened to pass by, but who said to me: "For the love of Christ, sir, give me a penny!" in a voice so harsh that I gave a start, overcome by some terrible feeling. I did not give him anything. I had not a penny on me. And yet rich people do not like to hear poor men complain aloud of their poor circumstances—they worry them, they are so importunate! Yes indeed, poor people are always importunate—their hungry moans interfere with the rich man's sleep!

I must tell you, my dear, that I began describing all this partly to get it off my chest, but also more particularly to give you an example of my excellent style. For I'm sure you will admit, dear heart, that my style has been improving lately. But at the moment, I'm in such a state of despondency that I'm beginning to sympathise deeply with my ideas, and though I realise very well that sympathy is not enough, it does—does it not?—to a certain extent do justice to my feelings. And, indeed, my dear, you all too often depreciate yourself, think little of yourself, value yourself less than dirt. But that, perhaps, is because I have been intimidated and been bullied myself just like—if I may draw such a comparison—the small boy who asked me for alms. Let me now tell you something in the nature of an allegory, dear heart. Now, listen, please. Early in the morning as I hurry to the office, I sometimes happen to cast a look at the city to see how it awakens, gets up, sends up wreaths of smoke, boils over, thunders—before such a spectacle you can't help feeling small, just as if someone gave a fillip to your inquisitive nose, and away you shuffle off quiet as a mouse and give it all up with a despairing wave of the hand. But, pray, take a good look at what is going on in those black, grimy, huge blocks of flats, think it over carefully and then judge for yourself whether it is right to depreciate oneself without rhyme or reason and feel embarrassed unnecessarily. Note, please, dearest Barbara, that I'm speaking figuratively and not literally. Well, let's see what is going on in those houses. There in some smoke-filled corner, in a damp hovel which is supposed to be a lodging, some tradesman awakes from sleep; all night he has been dreaming—shall we say?—of a pair of boots which the day before he had accidentally cut too low, as though a man had to dream of such rubbish. But he's a tradesman, a cobbler, and he can be forgiven for dreaming about his own work: he has screaming children and a hungry wife. And it is not only cobblers who sometimes get up like that, my dear. This may be of no interest and hardly worth writing about except for something else, dear heart. You see, in the same house, a story lower or higher, in gilt chambers, a very wealthy man is perhaps also dreaming at night of a pair of boots, I mean boots of a different kind, of a different fashion, but still of boots, for in the allegorical sense I am speaking of, we are all of us, dear heart, some sort of cobbler. That, too, would not matter, but what is wrong is that there is not a single man who could whisper in the rich man's ear: why think of such things? Why think only of yourself? Why live only for yourself? You are not a cobbler, your children are all well, and your wife does not beg for food. Look around you—can't you find a subject more worthy of your worries than your boots? That's what I want to tell you in allegorical language, dear Barbara. It may be I'm going a little too far, but such a thought exists, such a thought often occurs to me and it is then that it wells out of one's heart involuntarily in passionate words. That is why one should not think that one isn't worth more than a farthing because one is frightened of the roar and thunder of the city. Let me conclude, dear heart, by answering you that you are wrong if by any chance you think that I am casting aspersions on people, that I am saying all this because I feel depressed, or that I have copied it all out of a book. No, my dearest, I abhor slander, I am not suffering from depression, and I have not copied anything out of a book—no, madam!

I came home feeling sad, sat down at the table, brewed a pot of tea and was just about to have a glass or two when Gorshkov, our poor lodger, looked in. Already this morning I had noticed that he was hanging about the place and seemed to wish to have a talk with me. Let me tell you in passing, dear heart, that his circumstances are much worse than mine. No comparison! A wife, children! Indeed, if I were Gorshkov I don't know what I should do! Well, so Gorshkov came in, bowed, tears, as usual, trembling on his eyelashes, scraped his feet and was unable to utter a word. I asked him to sit down (the chair, it is true, was broken, but I had no other). Asked him to have some tea. He kept refusing at first, kept refusing for quite a long time, but at last accepted the offered glass. He would not accept any sugar, offering all sorts of excuses, while I tried my best to persuade him to take some; he went on arguing for a long time, insisting that he never had any sugar in his tea, but at last put a tiny lump of sugar in his glass and then kept telling me that his tea was very sweet. To such depths of humility does poverty reduce a man! "Well, sir," I said, "what can I do for you?" "You see," he replied, "my dear benefactor, Makar Alexeyevich, I've come to ask you to do me a great favour and help my unhappy family. My wife and children have nothing to eat and you can imagine what I, a father, am going through." I was about to say something, but he interrupted me. "You see, my dear sir, I'm afraid of everybody here. I mean, I'm not so much afraid as ashamed; they're all such a proud and conceited lot. I should not have bothered you myself, my dear sir, for I know that you have troubles of your own and I also know that you can't afford to give me much, but do lend me a little. I ventured to ask you," he said, "because I know how kind-hearted you are. I know that you have been in need and that you're in a terrible situation yourself and that's perhaps why you can sympathise with me in your heart." He concluded by apologising for his impertinence and impropriety. I told him that I'd be only too glad to help him, but that I had nothing, absolutely nothing myself. "But, my dear Mr. Devushkin," he said, "I'm not asking much, but you realise my position—a wife and children (at this point he blushed)—they are starving. Couldn't you let me have just ten copecks?" Here, I must confess, I felt sick at heart. Well, I thought, he certainly has outdone me all right! I had only twenty copecks left and I counted on them to meet my most urgent requirements. Well, so I took out my twenty copecks from my box and gave them to him—the lot, dear heart. A good deed, I suppose! Dear me, what poverty! We then had a long talk together. "How did you get into such a plight, my dear fellow?" I asked him. "And being in such awful straits, how could you rent a room at five silver roubles?" He told me that he had rented the room six months ago and had paid three months' rent in advance. After that his circumstances had taken a turn for the worse, and he did not know what to do, poor fellow. He had thought that his lawsuit would be finished by then. It's a very unpleasant business altogether. You see, Barbara, he is a defendant in a case in which a merchant is on trial for defrauding the Treasury. The fraud was discovered, the merchant was prosecuted, whereupon he involved Gorshkov, who happened to be somehow involved in his malpractices. Truth to tell, Gorshkov is only guilty of carelessness, imprudence and inexcusable neglect in failing to take proper care of the Treasury's interests. The case has now been dragging on for several years, and all sorts of difficulties have piled up against Gorshkov. "I am not guilty of the dishonourable conduct they accuse me of." Gorshkov told me. "I am not guilty, not guilty of theft and embezzlement!" The affair has damaged his reputation to some extent. Though he was not found absolutely guilty, he was dismissed from the service, but until he is pronounced entirely innocent, he cannot recover from the merchant the considerable amount of money owed to him, though disputed before the court. I believe him, but the court does not trust him. It's all so complicated and tangled that you won't sort it out in a hundred years. As soon as they disentangle one thing, the merchant ties something else up in a knot again. I'd like to help Gorshkov and I'm very sorry for him. He has no job, he can't get one because no one will trust him. They have spent everything they had saved. It's a complicated business and meantime—it could not have happened at a worse time—another child was born to them, and there are more expenses. A son got sick—expenses; he died—expenses; his wife is in bad health, he is suffering from some complaint of long standing. In short, he has been through a hell of a lot. Still, he says that he is expecting a favourable issue to his affair any day and that now he has no doubt of it whatsoever. I am sorry, very sorry for him, dear heart. I tried to be as nice to him as possible. He is a lost, muddled creature, looking for someone to stretch out a helping hand to him, so I was kind to him. Well, good-bye, dear heart. Christ be with you and keep you well. My darling, the moment I think of you, I feel as though I applied a medicine to my aching soul, and even if I suffer for you, I am happy to do so.

Your true friend,
Makar Devushkin.

September 9th.

Dear Barbara,

I am beside myself. I am terribly upset, for a most awful thing has happened. My head is whirling round. I feel as if everything about me is going round and round. Oh, my dear, the things I've got to tell you now! I don't think we had an inkling of it. No, I cannot say that I had no inkling of it. I did foresee it all. My heart felt it all coming. I even saw something of the kind in a dream.

This is what happened. I'll tell it to you without bothering about style, just as God puts it into my heart. I went to the office today. I came, sat down, and began writing. I ought to tell you, dear heart, that yesterday, too, I was writing. Well, anyway, yesterday Timofey Ivanovich came up to me and told me that the document I was copying was a very important one and had to be finished quickly. "Please, Makar Alexeyevich," he said to me, "copy it out clearly, quickly and carefully. It will have to be signed today." I must tell you, my angel, that I was not feeling at all well yes-

terday. I did not feel like bothering about anything: I
felt so depressed and cheerless; my heart was chilled,
my mind darkened. I was thinking all the time of you,
my poor darling. Well, so I began copying. I copied it
out cleanly and well, except that—I don't know how to
put it more precisely—it was as if the devil himself
confused me or it had been ordained by some mysterious fate, or it simply was just bound to happen,
—I left out a whole line! Goodness only knows what
one could make of it!—one could make no sense of it
at all! They were not in time with the document yesterday, so they presented it for signature to His
Excellency this morning. I arrived this morning at the
usual time without suspecting anything and sat down
next to Yemelyan Ivanovich. I think I ought to tell
you, my dear, that for some time past I have been
feeling doubly nervous and anxious. Lately I dared not
even look at people. The moment a chair creaked, I
became more dead than alive. I felt exactly the same
today: I crouched down on my seat, as quiet as a
mouse, afraid to breathe, so that Yefim Akimovich (a
brazen-faced ruffian the like of whom you will not meet
anywhere in the world) said in a loud voice so that
everyone could hear: "What are you sitting like that
for, Makar Alexeyevich? Got the willies?" And he
pulled such a face that everyone near me and him
rocked with laughter. They were laughing at me, of
course. And they went on and on! I stopped my ears
and closed my eyes and just sat there without stirring.
I invariably do that: it's the quickest way to be left
in peace. Suddenly I heard a noise, a commotion,
people running about. Did my ears deceive me? They
were calling me, summoning me, calling for Devushkin.

My heart began to tremble within me. I did not know myself what I was frightened of. All I knew was that never in my life had I been so frightened as I was then. I seemed to be glued to my chair, pretending not to have heard anything, as though it weren't me at all. But they were coming nearer and nearer. They were shouting in my ear: "Devushkin! Devushkin! Where is Devushkin?" I raised my eyes. Eustaphy Ivanovich stood before me. "Makar Alexeyevich," he said, "His Excellency wants to see you. Hurry! You've made a mess of the document!" That was the only thing he said, but that was enough, was it not, dear heart? I turned deathly pale, as cold as ice, bereft of all sensations, and went, feeling more dead than alive. I was led through one room, then another and a third, and then to His Excellency's office—there I was! I cannot give you an exact account of what I was thinking at that moment. There was His Excellency standing before me and all of them around him. I don't think I even bowed—forgot! I was so confounded that my lips were trembling and my knees were knocking together. And with good reason, dear heart. In the first place, I felt ashamed: I glanced into a mirror on the right, and what I saw there was enough to drive me out of my mind. Secondly, I had always contrived to efface myself, just as if I did not exist at all. I don't suppose His Excellency even knew of my existence. Though of course, he might have heard, in passing, that a man named Devushkin was in his department, but never bothered to inquire further into it.

He began angrily: "What made you do it, sir? Why didn't you take more care? An important document, wanted in a hurry, and you have made a mess of it.

How could you, sir?" Then His Excellency turned to Eustaphy Ivanovich. All I could hear were just a few words: "Negligence! No consideration! Causing unpleasantness!" I opened my mouth to say something. I wanted to apologise, but I couldn't. I wanted to run away but dared not make the attempt, and then, then, dear heart, something happened that even now I can hardly hold my pen in my hand for shame. A button of mine—the devil take it!—that was hanging by a thread, suddenly came off, broke away, bounced (I must have touched it accidentally), rattled and rolled off, damn it, straight to the feet of His Excellency— and this amid the general silence! That was my only justification, my once excuse, my only reply—all I had to say to His Excellency! The consequences were terrible! His Excellency at once turned his attention to my figure and my uniform. I remembered what I had seen in the mirror and rushed to retrieve my button. I seemed to have gone out of my mind! I bent down and was about to pick up my button, but it rolled away, it spun round, I could not grasp it, in short, I distinguished myself for my adroitness! Then I felt that my last remaining strength was leaving me, that all, all was lost! That all my reputation was lost, that I was done for! Suddenly, for no reason at all, my ears were filled with the chatter of Teresa and Faldoni—it went on and on! At last I caught the button, got up, straightened myself and, damn fool that I am, I ought to have stood there quietly at attention. But no! I began to attach the button to the torn threads, as though it could be attached to them, and I kept smiling as I did so. I kept smiling! At first, His Excellency turned away from me; then he glanced at me again. I heard him say to Eustaphy Ivanovich: "Good heavens, look at him! How has he got into such a state? Who is he?"

Well, my dear, how indeed? And who indeed! Distinguished myself, I have! I could hear Eustaphy Ivanovich saying: "He's never been in any trouble before . . . exemplary conduct . . . his salary's sufficient —according to scale." His Excellency said: "Try to make it easier for him. . . . Let him have some salary in advance." "He has drawn some for a considerable time in advance. I expect his circumstances made him ask for an advance, but his conduct is good and he has never been in trouble before—never." I felt as if I were burning, my angel, burning in hell-fire! I felt like dying! "Well," said His Excellency, "let him copy out the document as quickly as possible. Devushkin, come here. You are to copy it again without any mistakes. And look here—" He turned to the other officials, issued a few orders to them, and they all went out. As soon as they were gone, His Excellency hurriedly pulled out his wallet and took out a hundred rouble note. "Here," he said, "I'm afraid that's all I can afford. Treat it as you like." And he shoved it into my hand. I gave a start, my angel; I was shaken to the core. I don't know what happened to me, I wanted to grasp his hand, but he, the dear fellow, blushed and— I am not departing by a hair's breadth from the truth, my dear—took my unworthy hand and shook it. Yes, indeed, he took my hand and shook it just as if I had been his equal. "Go now," he said, "I'm afraid that's all I can do. . . . Don't make any more mistakes. I'll overlook this one. . . ."

Now, what I have decided is this, dear heart. I ask

you and Theodora, and if I had children, I should tell them also: you need not pray for your father, but you must pray every day for His Excellency forever! I have something else to tell you, my dear, and I'm saying it most solemnly—please, listen carefully: I swear that though I have nearly died of grief during these cruel days of our adversity at the sight of you and your misfortunes, at my own humiliation and incapacity, in spite of all that, I swear that it is not so much the hundred roubles that I appreciate as that His Excellency was good enough to shake the hand of a worthless drunkard like me. By this act he has restored me to myself. By this act he has resurrected my spirit, made life sweeter to me forever, and I am quite sure that, however great a sinner I may be before God, my prayer for the happiness and prosperity of His Excellency will reach His throne! . . .

Dear heart, I am now in a state of nervous agitation. My heart is pounding as though it would burst from my breast. I myself feel awfully weak for some reason. I send you forty-five roubles in notes. I shall give twenty roubles to my landlady and keep thirty-five roubles—twenty for mending my clothes and fifteen for living expenses. I'm afraid all these impressions of this morning have shaken me up so much that I must lie down. I feel at peace, though. Very much at peace. Except that my heart is uneasy—deep, deep inside I feel it trembling, quivering, stirring. I'll come to see you. Now I'm simply drunk with all these sensations. . . . God sees all things, dear heart, my priceless darling!

Your sincere friend,
Makar Devushkin.

September 10th.

My dear Mr. Devushkin,

I am terribly glad at your good fortune and I greatly appreciate the goodness of your chief, my friend. So now you can take a rest from your troubles. Only for goodness' sake don't waste your money again. Live quietly, as frugally as possible, from today, try to save up something so as not to be suddenly overtaken by disaster again. Please do not worry about us. Theodora and I will manage somehow. And why did you send us so much money? We do not need it. We are quite satisfied with what we have. True, we shall soon need some money to move to other lodgings, but Theodora is hoping to receive repayment of an old debt. I'm keeping twenty roubles, though, for urgent necessities. The rest I am returning to you. Please, take good care of your money, Mr. Devushkin. Good-bye. Don't worry, keep well and be of good cheer. I'd have written more, but I'm terribly tired. I stayed in bed all day yesterday. I'm glad you've promised to come and see me. Do come, please, Mr. Devushkin.

B.D.

September 11th.

My dear Barbara,

I implore you, my dear, not to leave me now that I am so happy and contented. My darling, don't listen to Theodora. I'll do anything for you: I'll behave, even if only out of respect for His Excellency, and I promise to give a good account of myself. We shall again write happy letters to each other and confide our thoughts to each other as well as our joys and troubles, if we should have any more troubles. Let us live in peace and harmony. Let us do a lot of reading. My angel, a great change has taken place in my life, a change for the better. My landlady has become more accommodating, Teresa more intelligent, and even Faldoni somehow shows greater willingness. I have made my peace with Ratazyaev. As a mark of my good fortune, I went to see him myself. He really is a good fellow, dear heart, and the bad things they said about him is all nonsense. I have now discovered that it was all just an odious slander. He had no intention of putting us into a book: he told me so himself. He read to me his new work. As for calling me "Lovelace," he explained to me that it was not an abusive or indecent name. The word is of foreign derivation and it means a fellow who knows what he is about or, to put it better and in more literary language, a fellow who does not lead anyone into temptation. That's what it means and not anything—well—not quite proper. It was just a harmless joke, my angel. Ignoramus that I am, I foolishly took offence without cause. I have offered my apologies to him now. The weather is so lovely today, Barbara. Such glorious weather! True, this morning there was sleet and rain as though scattered through a sieve. Never mind! The air was much fresher because of it. I went out to buy myself some boots and bought a marvellous pair. Then I went for a stroll on Nevsky Avenue. I read the *Northern Bee*. Good heavens, I've forgotten to tell you the most important thing of all!

You see, what happened is this:

This morning I had a long talk about His Excellency with Yemelyan Ivanovich and Aksenty Mikhailovich. Well, dear Barbara, I am not the only one he has

treated with such kindness. I am not the only one to
whom he has been so charitable. The whole world
knows his goodness of heart. His praises can be heard
in many quarters where tears of gratitude are shed.
He brought up an orphan girl and married her to a
man of good position, a civil servant attached to his
own department as an official on special duties. He
found a position for a widow's son in some government office and is well known for many other benefactions. I, too, thought it to be my duty, dear heart,
to add my mite by telling them all of His Excellency's treatment of me, without concealing anything.
I pocketed pride, for what is there I should be ashamed
of or put on airs about in a case like this? I told them
about it in a loud voice—let the actions of His Excellency be glorified! I spoke with enthusiasm, excitedly,
without blushing. On the contrary, I felt proud to
have such a story to tell. I told them everything,
except, of course, mentioning you, dear heart. I told
them about my landlady, about Faldoni, about
Ratazyaev, about my boots and about Markov—I told
them everything. Some of them exchanged smiles. I
expect they must have found something comical about
my figure or the story of my boots—yes, I think it must
have been my boots. They could not possibly have
done so with any evil intent. I suppose it must be their
youth or the fact that they are rich men, they certainly
could not have been laughing at what I told them with
any evil intent. I mean, so far as His Excellency is concerned—they could not possibly have done that! Don't
you think so, Barbara?

I still can't come to my senses, dear heart. All these
events have completely confused me. Have you enough

fuel? Don't catch a cold, Barbara. It doesn't take very long to catch a cold, does it? Oh, dear heart, your melancholy thoughts do cast a gloom over me. I pray to God, oh, how I pray to Him for you, dear heart! I mean, have you any woollen stockings or any warm clothes? Please, darling, if you need anything, don't hurt an old man's feelings, for God's sake, but come straight to me. The bad times are over now. Don't worry about me. Everything ahead is bright and beautiful.

We have certainly been through hard times, Barbara. Well, never mind. It's all over. As the years pass we shall remember, too, with a sigh of relief. I still remember the years of my youth. Good Lord, sometimes I did not have a copeck to spare. Cold and hungry, I kept cheerful all the same. I'd have a stroll along Nevsky Avenue in the morning, come across a pretty face and feel happy all day. It was glorious, a glorious time, dear heart. It's good to be alive, Barbara. Especially in Petersburg. I was beseeching God with tears in my eyes yesterday to forgive me my sins during that sorrowful time: my murmurings, my liberal ideas, my debaucheries and my gambling. I remembered you in my prayers with tender emotion. You alone, my angel, have given me strength. You alone have comforted me, given me good advice and instruction. I shall never forget that, dear heart. I have kissed all your letters today, my darling. Well, good-bye, dear heart. I'm told that there's going to be a sale of second-hand clothing not far from here. I'll go and have a look. Good-bye again, my angel. Good-bye.

Yours ever devoted,
Makar Devushkin.

September 15th.

Dear Mr. Devushkin,

I am terribly upset. I can't help feeling that something awful is going to happen. Judge for yourself, dearest friend. Mr. Bykov is in Petersburg. Theodora has met him. He was driving along, stopped the cab, walked up to Theodora and asked her where she was living. At first she would not tell him. Then he said with a smile that he knew whom she was living with. (Anna Fyodorovna must have told him everything.) It was then that Theodora could not hold out any longer and right there in the street began reproaching and upbraiding him. She told him that he was a man without morals and that he was the cause of all my misfortunes. He replied that it was only natural if one hadn't a penny, one was unhappy. Theodora told him that I could have lived by my work, or could have married or found some post, but that now I had lost my happiness forever and, moreover, was ill and might soon die. To which he replied that I was still quite young, that my head was still full of all sorts of silly notions and that our "virtues, too, have lost their lustre" (his very words). Theodora and I had thought that he did not know where we lived, when, suddenly, last night, just after I left to do some shopping in the Arcade, he came in (he had apparently not wanted to find me at home). He asked Theodora many questions about our way of living, examined everything carefully, inspected my work, and at last asked: "Who is this civil servant you seem to know?" At that moment you happened to walk across the courtyard. Theodora pointed you out: he looked at you and grinned. Theodora implored him to go. She told him that I was still

ill from worry and that I would be greatly upset to see
him there. He was silent for a while; then he said he
merely looked in because he had nothing else to do. He
wanted to give Theodora twenty-five roubles, but of
course she would not accept the money. What could it
mean? Why has he come to see us? I can't understand
how he could have got all this information about us. I
am lost in conjecture. Theodora says that Aksinya, her
sister-in-law, who visits us, knows the laundress, Nastasya and that Nastasya's cousin is a porter in the department in which a friend of Anna Fyodorovna's
nephew is employed. Is it possible that some kind of
scandalous story has come from there? Still, it is quite
possible that Theodora is mistaken. We don't know
what to think. He will not come again, will he?
The very thought horrifies me. When Theodora told
me all this last night, I got so terrified that I nearly
fainted. What more do they want? I don't want to
know them! What have they to do with a poor creature
like me? Oh dear, I am now in such a state of appre-
hension. I am expecting Bykov to come in any moment.
What will become of me? What more has Fate in store
for me? For Christ's sake, come and see me at once,
Mr. Devushkin. For God's sake, come!

B.D.

September 18th.

Dear heart,

A most grievous, unexpected and utterly inexplicable occurrence took place today in our house. Our
poor Gorshkov, I ought to tell you, dear heart, has
been completely exonerated. The decision had been
given some time ago, but this morning he went to

hear the court's final verdict. The case concluded very
happily for him. Whatever blame he might have incurred for his negligence and imprudence—he was
completely exonerated on all counts. The merchant
has been ordered to pay him a large sum of money,
so that his circumstances have greatly improved, and
every blot on his reputation has been wiped out and
everything has changed for the better—in short, his
wishes have been completely fulfilled. He returned
home at three o'clock. He looked awful, pale as a sheet,
his lips were trembling, but there was a smile on them
and he embraced his wife and children. We all went
trooping into his room to congratulate him. He was
deeply touched by our action, bowed to us, and shook
each of us by the hand several times. It seemed to me
even that he had grown taller, that he had straightened out, and that there were no longer any tears in
his eyes. He was terribly excited, poor fellow. He
could not stand still for two minutes. He kept picking
things up and dropping them again. He smiled incessantly and bowed, sat down, got up, sat down again
and goodness only knows what he kept talking about.
"My honour," he kept saying, "my good name, my children . . ." and how he talked! He even burst into
tears. We, too, mark you, shed a few tears. Ratazyaev,
wishing probably to cheer him up, said: "My dear
sir, what's the use of honour if you have nothing to
eat. Money, sir, is the chief thing—money! That's
what we have to thank the Lord for!" And he patted
his shoulder. I thought Gorshkov looked hurt, not
that he showed any displeasure, but he gave Ratazyaev
a rather strange look and removed his hand from his
shoulder. He would never have done that before, dear

heart. Still, characters differ. I myself, for instance, would not have betrayed any pride on such a joyful occasion. Why, my dear, sometimes another bow and a show of humility is the result of an excess of goodness of heart and gentle disposition . . . but then this has nothing to do with me. "Yes, indeed," Gorshkov said, "money's a great thing too, thank God, thank God!" And the whole time we remained with him, he kept repeating: "Thank God, thank God!" His wife ordered a larger and more delectable dinner. Our landlady cooked it for them herself. She isn't really such a bad woman. Before dinner Gorshkov could not keep still. He went to every room, whether invited or not. He would just go in, smile, sit down on a chair, sometimes say something and sometimes not utter a word—and go out. In the midshipman's room he even picked up some playing cards. He was invited to make a fourth in the game. He joined the players, made a mess of their game, and after two or three moves gave it up. "Sorry," he said, "I didn't really, you know, I didn't really mean to . . ." and went out. He came across me in the corridor, took hold of both my hands, looked me straight in the eye, only in a rather funny sort of way; then he pressed my hand and went off, smiling all the time, but rather wearily, strangely as though he were dead. His wife was weeping for joy. Everything in their room was so gay, just as if it were some holiday. Dinner was soon over. After dinner Gorshkov said to his wife: "I think I'll take a little nap, darling," and he went to bed. He called his little daughter, put his hand on her head and kept stroking the child's head a long time. Then he again turned to his wife and said: "What about little Peter? Our little Peter?" His

wife crossed herself and replied that little Peter was
dead. "Yes," he said, "I know, I know everything. Peter's now in the Kingdom of Heaven." His wife, who
realised that he was not himself, that what had happened had shaken him to the core, said to him: "You'd
better try to sleep, darling." "Very well, I will—a little," he replied, turning over and lying still for a time.
Then he turned round again, wanted to say something, but his wife did not catch what he was saying.
She asked him: "What is it?" but he did not reply. She
waited a little, thought that he was asleep, and went to
spend an hour chatting with the landlady. When she
returned, she saw that her husband had not yet woken
up and was lying still without stirring. Thinking that
he was asleep, she sat down and began to do some
work. She told us that she had been working for about
half an hour and had sunk so deep in thought that she
could not remember what she was thinking of, except
that she seemed to have completely forgotten about
her husband. Then she suddenly came to with a kind
of uneasy feeling. The first thing that struck her was
the death-like stillness in the room. Glancing at the
bed, she saw that her husband was still lying in the
same position as before. She went up to him, pulled
down the blanket and perceived that he had already
gone cold. He was dead, dear heart, Gorshkov had
died suddenly, just as if he had been struck by lightning. Goodness only knows what he died of. I am so
shocked by it, dearest, that I can't yet collect myself.
I just can't believe that a man could die like that.
What a poor, wretched fellow that Gorshkov was!
What a fate, what a fate! His wife is in tears and looks
frightened. His little daughter is hiding in some cor-

ner. There is such confusion there. There's going to be a post mortem. I can't tell you anything for certain . . . except that I feel so sorry, so sorry for them. It is sad to think that you never can tell what a day, what an hour can bring. . . . You just perish like that for nothing. . . .

Yours,
Makar Devushkin.

September 19th.

My dear Barbara,

I hasten to inform you that my friend Ratazyaev has found me some work to do for a certain writer. The writer called on him and left a very large manuscript —thank God, there's plenty of work. But the handwriting is so difficult to decipher that I don't know how to set about copying it. He wants it done as soon as possible. Besides, it is so obscure that one can scarcely understand what it is all about. We agreed about my fee—forty copecks a sheet. I am writing you all this, my dear, to let you know that now I can count on some additional income. Well, good-bye, dear heart. I must set to work.

Your true friend,
Makar Devushkin.

September 23rd.

My dear friend,

I have not written to you during the last three days because I have been greatly worried and upset.

Bykov came to see me three days ago. I was alone; Theodora had gone out somewhere. I answered the door and was so terrified when I saw him that I stood

rooted to the spot. I felt that I had turned pale. He
came in laughing loudly, as usual, took a chair, and
sat down. For a long time I could not collect myself,
but at last I sat down in my corner of the room and
went on with my work. He stopped laughing soon.
He seemed to have been struck by my appearance. I
have grown so thin lately, my eyes and cheeks have
grown hollow, and I was as pale as a sheet. Anyone
who knew me a year ago would really find it difficult
to recognise me. He looked intently at me for a long
time, but soon regained his high spirits. He said something. I don't remember what I replied, but he
laughed again. He spent a whole hour with me, talked
to me a great deal, and put some questions to me. At
last, before leaving, he took me by the hand and said
(I am quoting his very words): "My dear Barbara, between ourselves, Anna Fyodorovna, your relation and
my good friend and acquaintance, is a villainous old
woman. (He also called her a most offensive name.)
She led your cousin astray and she ruined you. So far
as I am concerned, I must admit that I behaved like a
scoundrel, but then such is life! . . ." At this, he
burst out laughing at the top of his voice. Then he
observed that he was no fine speaker and that, above
all, he had to explain himself, which, indeed, he felt it
to be his duty as a gentleman not to pass in silence.
He would, therefore, come straight to the point, as
briefly as possible. He then told me that he was asking
me for my hand in marriage, that he thought it to be
his duty to make an honest woman of me, that he was
a wealthy man, that after our wedding he would take
me to his country estate in the steppes, where he
would hunt hares, that he would never return to Pe-

tersburg, because Petersburg was a rotten city and because he had a nephew there who, he said, was a worthless fellow whom he wished to disinherit, and that it was for that very reason he wanted to marry me, as he wished to have legal heirs. That was the chief reason why he proposed to me. He next remarked that I was living in very straitened circumstances and that it was, therefore, not surprising that I was ill, lodging as I did in such a hovel, that I would most certainly die within a month if I remained in such a place, that all lodgings in Petersburg were dreadful and, finally, that he would like to know whether I was in need of anything.

I was so amazed at his proposal that I could not help bursting into tears. He interpreted my tears as a sign of gratitude and said that he had always known I was a good, sensitive and well-educated girl, but that he had all the same made up his mind to take this step only after he had learned all the details of my present situation. Then he asked me about you, said that he had heard that you were a man of upright principles, that for his part he did not wish to remain in debt to you and would five hundred roubles be enough to recompense you for all you had done for me. When I told him that what you had done for me could not be repaid in money, he said that it was stuff and nonsense, that it was the sort of thing you read about in novels, that I was young and fond of poetry, that novels were the ruination of young girls, that books only corrupted morals, and that he could not abide books; that I had to live as long as he had before talking about people. "Then," he added, "you will learn what people are like." He went on to say that I should consider his proposal carefully, that he would not like me to take such an important step without thinking it over, adding that thoughtlessness and enthusiasm led to the ruin of inexperienced youth, but that he was extremely anxious to receive a favourable reply from me. Otherwise he would be forced to marry a merchant's daughter in Moscow, for he had vowed to disinherit that scoundrel of a nephew of his. In spite of my protest, he left five hundred roubles on my embroidery frame to buy myself sweets, as he put it. He told me that I'd get as plump as a dumpling, that I'd live in clover, that he was very busy just now, that he'd been running about on business all day, and that he'd run in to see me between one business deal and another. Then he went away. I have thought things over for a long time, worrying and feeling unhappy, and at last I've made up my mind. My friend, I'm going to marry him. I have to accept his proposal. If anyone could save me from my disgrace, restore my good name and avert poverty, hardships and misfortunes from me in the future, he is the only man to do so. What can I expect from the future? What more have I to ask for? Theodora says that one ought not to lose sight of one's happiness. She says—what else is one to call happiness in a case like this? I, at any rate, cannot, my dear, dear, friend, find any other way for me. What else can I do? I go on working as it is and have ruined my health as a result. I cannot go on working forever. Get a post as a governess? I'm sure I shall waste away with grief, and, besides, I shall not please anybody. I am sickly by nature and shall, therefore, always be a burden to other people. I realise, of course, that my married life won't be a paradise, but what am I to do, my friend? What *am* I to do? Have I any other choice?

I did not ask your advice. I wanted to think it over myself. My decision, which you have just read, is unalterable. I shall communicate it at once to Bykov, who is pressing me for my final answer, as it is. He told me that his business deals could not wait, that he had to leave and that he was not going to delay them for something that was of no importance. God knows whether I shall be happy, my future is in His sacred, inscrutable hands, but I have made up my mind. I am told that Bykov is a kind-hearted man. He will respect me. Perhaps I will respect him also. What more is one to expect from our marriage?

I have now told you everything. I am sure you will understand my distress. Do not try to dissuade me from my decision. Your efforts will be in vain. Weigh up in your own heart what has forced me to take this step. I was terribly upset at first, but now I feel more calm. What the future holds for me I don't know. What will be, will be. Whatever God may send . . .

Bykov has just arrived. I am leaving this letter unfinished. I'd like to have said a lot more to you. Bykov is here!

B.D.

September 23rd.

My darling Barbara,

I hasten to reply to you, dear heart. I hasten to tell you that I am dumbfounded. The whole thing, somehow, doesn't sound right. Yesterday we buried Gorshkov. Yes indeed, my dear. Yes indeed! Bykov has acted honourably. So, you see, my dear, you *have* given your consent. No doubt, God's will is in everything. It is so, it must be so, I mean, in this, too. There must be an indication of God's will in this, and the purposes of the Heavenly Father must be both beneficial and inscrutable, as it is also of Fate, which is one and the same. Theodora, too, is thinking of your interest. Of course, you will be happy now, dear heart. You will live in comfort, my darling, my sweet angel—only, my dear, why all this haste? Well, of course, business—Mr. Bykov has all sorts of business deals—who hasn't? He, too, may have some. . . . I caught a glimpse of him as he was leaving your house. A handsome man, a very handsome man, indeed! Only something does not seem right. . . . What matters is not that he is a handsome man—I'm afraid that I'm not quite myself now. What worries me is how we shall be able to write letters to each other. How am I to be left alone? You see, my angel, I keep weighing up, weighing up the reasons as you have written to me, I keep weighing them up in my heart. . . . I was just finishing the twentieth page of my copying when this had to happen. Now that you're going away, you will have to be making all sorts of purchases, all sorts of shoes, dresses, so—well—as it happens I know of a shop in Gorokhavaya Street—I described it to you, remember? But, good heavens—no! How can you go to the country now? It's impossible. Quite impossible. You have to buy so many things, and acquire a carriage. Besides, the weather's bad at present: just look: it's raining cats and dogs, such soaking rain, too, and, besides, my angel, besides, you will be cold, your heart will be cold. . . . You see, you're afraid of strangers, and yet you're going away. . . . And what about me? I'll be left alone here. Theodora says that great happiness is awaiting you, but then she's a savage, peasant woman and she wants to ruin me. Will you be going to evening mass today, dear heart? I'd like to come to see you. It's, of course, absolutely true, dear heart, that you're an educated, virtuous and sensitive girl, but I'd rather he married the merchant's daughter. What do you think, dear heart? Yes, he'd far better marry the merchant's daughter. I'll come and see you for an hour as soon as it grows dark, Barbara, my dear. It's getting dark early now, so I'll look in. Yes, dear heart, I'll most certainly see you for an hour today. You're expecting Bykov now, and I'll come in as soon as he's gone. Wait for me, dear heart, I'll run in for a moment. . . .

Makar Devushkin.

September 27th.

My dear friend,

Mr. Bykov tells me that I simply must have at least three dozen fine linen chemises. So I must find a seamstress as soon as possible to make two dozen, for we have very little time left. Mr. Bykov is angry. He says these fripperies cause much too much fuss. There are only five days left before our wedding, and we shall be leaving the day after. Mr. Bykov is in a great hurry, and he says that we should not waste much time on such trifles. All this rushing about has tired me out, and I can hardly stand on my feet. There's so much to do, and I really can't help thinking that it would be better if nothing of it were necessary. And another thing: I haven't enough silk and other lace, so I have to buy some, for Mr. Bykov says that he does not want his wife to walk about looking like a cook, and I simply

must "put the noses of all the wives of the gentry out
of joint." That's how he expressed it. So, please, Mr.
Devushkin, go to Madame Chiffon's, in Gorokhavaya
Street, and ask her, first of all, to send me some seamstress and, secondly, to be so good as to come and see
me herself. I am not feeling well today. Our new flat is
very cold, and everything there is in a terrible mess.
Bykov's aunt is so old she can hardly draw breath,
and I'm afraid she may die before we leave. But Mr.
Bykov says I'm not to worry as she will soon recover.
Everything here is in an awful mess. Mr. Bykov does
not live with us, so the servants are constantly running
off goodness knows where. Quite often Theodora
alone waits on us. Mr. Bykov's valet, who should be
keeping an eye on everything, has been missing for
three days. Mr. Bykov comes to see us every morning.
He's always in a temper and yesterday he was in trouble with the police because he had thrashed the man-
ager of the house. I have no one to send this letter to
you by. I am sending it by the city mail. Heavens, I
had nearly forgotten the most important thing. Tell
Madame Chiffon that I want her to change the silk
lace to match yesterday's pattern and that she should
come herself and show me her new selection. And,
tell her, please, that I have changed my mind about
the sleeveless light coat and that I'd like it to be
trimmed with crochet-work. One more thing: the
monograms on the handkerchiefs are to be embroi-
dered on a tambour—you understand?—on a tambour
and not in satin stitch. So, please, do not forget that
it's to be on a tambour. Good heavens, I nearly forgot: tell her that the lappets on the cape should be

raised, the different patterns *cordonné*, and the collar
to be trimmed with lace or a wide *falbala*. Please, tell
her that, dear Mr. Devushkin.

Yours,
B.D.

P.S. I am ashamed to worry you with my commissions.
The day before yesterday, too, you spent the whole
morning running about on my behalf. But what can
I do? Our whole house is in disorder, and I'm not feeling well myself. So, please, don't be vexed with me,
dear Mr. Devushkin. I'm in such a state! And what's
to become of me, my dear, dear friend? I'm afraid to
look into the future! I have a kind of foreboding and I
seem to live in a kind of daze.
P.P.S. For God's sake, my friend, do not forget anything I've just mentioned to you. I'm so afraid that
you might make some mistake. Remember, please: on
a tambour and not in satin stitch.

September 27th.

My dear Barbara,

I have zealously carried out all your commissions.
Madame Chiffon tells me that she herself had thought
of edging the border on the tambour, that it was more
elegant or something—I'm afraid I didn't quite catch
the gist of her words. As for the *falbala* you mentioned, she said something about that, too, but I'm
afraid I have quite forgotten what she said about it.
All I remember is that she talked a lot. What a horrible woman! What else? Why, she'll tell you everything herself. I'm sorry, dear heart, but I'm fagged out.
I haven't even gone to the office today. But you, my

dear, have no reason to despair. I'm ready to visit every shop in town to save you from worry. You write that you're afraid to look into the future. But tonight at seven o'clock you will learn everything. Madame Chiffon will come to see you in person. So don't despair, hope for the best, dear heart, perhaps everything will be for the best. Yes, indeed. I'm still worried about that damn *falbala*. Oh, that *falbala*, *falbala*! I'd have come to see you, my angel. Truly, I would. Why, I've walked past the gates of your house twice today! But that Bykov, I mean, Mr. Bykov, is always in such a bad temper, and that's why I didn't . . . oh, well, never mind!

M.D.

September 28th.

My darling Barbara,

I—that is, the jeweller says it's all right. As for me, I merely wanted to tell you that I have fallen ill and cannot get up from bed. It would happen just now at such a busy time when so many things have to be done that I'd go and catch a chill, the devil take it! I must also inform you that in addition to all my troubles His Excellency, too, has grown strict and was angry with, and shouted at, Yemelyan Ivanovich, and that he, poor fellow, was quite exhausted at the end. I thought I'd better tell you all that. There's something else I wanted to tell you, but I'm afraid to trouble you. You see, dear heart, I am a foolish, simple man. I write what happens to enter my head, so you might for all I know . . . well, never mind!

Your Makar Devushkin.

September 29th.

My dear, dear Barbara,

Today, my dearest, I saw Theodora. She tells me that you are to be married tomorrow and that you are leaving the day after. Mr. Bykov has already hired a carriage. I have already told you about His Excellency, dear heart. Another thing: I have checked the bills from the shop in Gorokhavaya Street: they are correct, except that it's all very expensive. Only why is Mr. Bykov angry with you? Well, I hope you will be happy, dear heart. I am glad. I shall be very glad if you are happy. I'd have liked to come to the church, dear heart, but I'm afraid I can't because of the pain in the small of my back. Well, as to our letters, I don't suppose there will be anyone now to send them by, will there, dear heart? I'm so glad you've done so much for Theodora. You've done a good deed, my dear. That was well done. A good deed! The Lord will bless you for every good deed. Good deeds do not go unrewarded, and charity is always crowned by divine justice, sooner or later. I'd have liked to write a lot to you —every hour, every minute I should have liked to write to you! I've still got a book of yours—*The Tales of Belkin*. You know, don't you, dear heart? So, please, don't take it away. Give it to me as a present, my dear. It isn't because I want to read it so much. But, as you know very well, winter is coming, the evenings will be long, I shall be feeling sad, so at least I shall have something to read. I intend to move from my lodgings, dear heart, into your old ones, which I shall rent from Theodora. I shall never part from that honest woman now. Besides, she is such an excellent worker. I inspected your empty room carefully yesterday. There's

still your embroidery frame there with some of your
work. It's been left untouched in its corner. I examined your embroidery. A few bits and pieces are still
left. On one of my letters you had begun winding
some thread. In the drawer of the table I found a few
bits of paper; on one of them you had written: "Dear
Mr. Devushkin, I'm in a hurry"—that was all. I suppose someone must have interrupted you at that very
tantalizing place. In the corner behind the screen is
your little bed. . . . My darling!!! Well, good-bye,
good-bye. For God's sake, send me something in reply
to this letter as soon as possible.

Makar Devushkin.

September 30th.

My dearest friend,

It is all over. The die is cast. I don't know what's in
store for me, but I submit to God's will. We are leaving tomorrow. I am saying good-bye to you for the
last time, my dear, dear friend, my benefactor. Do not
grieve for me, live happily, remember me, and may
God bless you. I shall often remember you in my
thoughts and in my prayers. So this time has come to
an end. I shall bring little joy into my new life from
the memories of my past. All the more precious will
be the memory of you, all the more precious will you
be in my heart. Here you alone have been my friend.
Here you alone have loved me. You see, I knew everything, I knew that you loved me. My smile was enough,
one line of a letter of mine was enough to make you
happy. You will have to try to forget me now. How
will you manage here by yourself? Who am I leaving
you to here, my good, my dearest, my only friend? I

am leaving you my book, my embroidery frame, and this letter which I have just begun. When you look on these lines, you must read more into them in your mind—everything you would have liked to hear or read from me, everything I would have written to you, and what would I not have written now! Remember your poor little Barbara who loved you so much. All your letters are in the top drawer of Theodora's chest of drawers. You write that you are ill, but Mr. Bykov does not let me go out anywhere today. I will write to you, my friend, I promise, but only God knows what may happen. So we'd better say good-bye now forever, my dearest, my dear, dear friend—forever! Oh, how warmly I'd have embraced you now! Good-bye, my friend, good-bye! Be happy, be well. I shall always pray for you. Oh, how sad I am, how heavy my heart! Mr. Bykov is calling me.

Your ever loving

B.

P.S. My heart is so full, so full of tears now.
My tears are choking me, are tearing me apart. Good-bye.
Oh dear, how sad!
Remember, remember your poor Barbara.

Dear heart, darling Barbara, my precious one, you are being taken away, you are leaving! I'd much rather they tore my heart out of my breast than take you away from me! How could you do it? You are crying and yet you are going away? I have just received your letter, it is all stained with your tears. So you do not want to leave, so you must be taken away by force, so

you are sorry for me, so you do love me. So what are
you going to do now? Who are you going to be with?
There your heart will be sad, sick and cold. It will
wither with anguish, it will break in half with grief.
You will die there, you will be laid to rest in the cold,
damp earth. There will be no one there even to shed
tears for you! Mr. Bykov will be hunting hares all the
time. Oh, dear heart, dear heart, how could you have
taken such a step, how could you do it? Oh, what have
you done, what have you done, what have you done to
yourself! Why, they'll bring you to your grave there,
they'll kill you there, my little angel. Why, you're as
weak as a feather! And where was I? Where were my
eyes, fool that I am? I could see that the child was
getting silly ideas into her head, that she was just
having a headache. I should have done something, but
instead, like a born fool, I did nothing, I saw nothing,
thought of nothing, just as if I were right in thinking
that it was none of my business—ran about to buy
some *falbalas!* Oh no, Barbara, I can't leave it like
that! I'm going to get up. I shall be better tomorrow,
perhaps, so I shall be able to get up! I shall throw myself under the wheels of your carriage—I shan't let you
go! And, indeed, why should such a thing be allowed?
What right have people to do such a thing? I shall go
with you. I'll run after your carriage if you won't take
me, and I shall go on running as fast as I can till I
collapse, gasping for breath. Do you realise what it is
like where you are going? Perhaps you don't, so you
had better ask me. The steppes, the bare steppes, as
bare as the palm of my hand, that's what it is like
there. A brutish peasant woman, an illiterate peasant,

drunkards—that's what the people there are like. By now the leaves have fallen off the trees there, it's raining, always raining there, it's cold there—and that's where you are going! Well, Mr. Bykov will be busy there—he will be hunting the hare, but what will you be doing? Do you want to be a squire's lady, dear heart? But, my darling angel, just take a good look at yourself. Do you look like a squire's lady? How could a thing like that have happened to you, Barbara? Who am I to write letters to, dear heart? Ah, yes, just think of that, dear heart—who is he going to write letters to? Who am I going to call "dear heart," who am I going to call by those affectionate words? Where am I to find you afterwards, my angel? I shall die, Barbara, I shall most certainly die: my heart will not be able to bear such a misfortune! I loved you like the light of God, I loved you like my own daughter, I loved everything about you, dear heart. I lived for you alone. I worked, I copied papers, I walked, I enjoyed myself, I wrote down my observations in the form of letters to a friend, and I did all that simply because you, dear heart, lived here, opposite, within reach. You did not perhaps know that, but that's how it was! Anyway, listen, dear heart, please, think carefully, my sweet darling, how can you possibly be leaving me? Why, my dear, you can't go, it's quite impossible for you to go, quite impossible! It's raining now, and you've such a delicate constitution, you're sure to catch a cold. Your carriage will get soaked through and through. Quite certain to get soaked. It will break down as soon as you drive past the city boundary: sure to break down. You see, in Petersburg, they don't know how to make decent carriages. I know these local carriage-builders very well: all they are after is to make something fashionable, something looking like a toy, but it won't last. I'll take my oath on it: it won't last. I'll throw myself on my knees to Mr. Bykov, dear heart: I'll prove it to him, I'll prove it all to him! You must prove it to him, too, reason with him, tell him that you are staying and that you cannot go! Why did he not marry the merchant's daughter in Moscow? He should have married her! A merchant's daughter was a much better match for him—I've good reason to say that! I'd have kept you here then. What do you want that Bykov for, dear heart? Why did he suddenly become so dear to you? Was it because he was buying you that *falbala*? But what's so marvellous about *falbalas*? Why *falbalas*? It's just rubbish, dear heart! Here it's a matter of life and death, and that is just a rag—*falbala* is! A rag, that's what your *falbala* is, dear heart. Why, as soon as I get my salary, I'll buy you lots of *falbalas*. I'll buy them for you, dear heart: you see, I know a little shop where they sell these frills and flounces: all you have to do is wait till I get my salary, my angel Barbara. Oh dear, oh dear, so you are going away to the steppes with Mr. Bykov, going away never to return. Oh, dear heart! You must write me one more letter, write me about everything, and when you're gone, you must write to me again from there. For else, my heavenly angel, this will be the last letter and yet it cannot possibly be our last letter. I mean, how can it be? So suddenly, so definitely—the last letter! No, no! I shall write to you and you must write to me. My style, too, you see, is just about to be formed. Oh, my dear, what does style matter? I hardly know what I am writing now. I simply don't know, I don't know anything, and I'm not going to read it again. I'm writing just for the sake of writing so that I can go on writing as long as possible. . . . Oh, my dearest, my darling, my dear heart!

A LITTLE HERO

FROM ANONYMOUS MEMOIRS

I was nearly eleven at the time. In July I had been sent to spend a holiday on an estate near Moscow owned by TV, a relative of mine, whose country-house was full of guests, fifty or perhaps more. . . . I don't remember, I didn't count. It was a noisy and gay party. It seemed as though it had been begun with the intention of going on forever. It seemed as though our host had pledged his word to squander his entire huge fortune as rapidly as possible which, indeed, he succeeded in doing not so long ago, that is to say, squandering all he possessed completely, to the last penny, to the last chip of wood. New guests kept arriving every minute. Moscow was within a stone's throw, in sight, so that those who left merely made room for others, and the party went on without interruption. Entertainments succeeded one another, and there seemed no end to the fun. Riding parties to the surrounding countryside; walks to the pine forest and along the river; picnics; *alfresco* dinners; supper on the large terrace, surrounded by rows of rare and costly flowers, which filled the fresh night air with their fragrance, and brilliantly illuminated, which made our ladies, who were almost without exception pretty anyhow, still more charming with their faces excited by the impressions of the day, their sparkling eyes, and their interchange of vivacious conversation intermingled with peals of ringing laughter; dances, music, songs; if the sky were overcast, tableaux vivants, charades, proverbs were arranged, amateur theatricals were organised. There were clever conversationalists, *raconteurs*, and wits among the guests.

There were also several persons who were more prominent among the other guests. There was, of course, a great deal of tittle-tattle and scandal, for the world could not exist without it and millions of people would have died like flies from sheer boredom. But as I was only eleven, I did not notice those people at the time, my interest being otherwise engaged, and even if I did notice something, it was not all. It was afterwards that I happened to remember certain things. At the time it was only the brilliant aspect of the picture that impressed my childish eyes, and the general excitement, the splendour, and the noise—all that hitherto unseen and unheard of struck me so much that during the first few days I was completely stunned and my little head was in a whirl.

But I go on speaking of my age and, of course, I was a mere child, no more than a child. When caressing me, many of those beautiful women never thought it necessary to ask me how old I was. But, strange to say, a feeling which I could not comprehend myself had taken possession of me, something already set my heart aflutter, something that till that visit was unfamiliar and unknown to it, but which sometimes made it throb and burn as though it were frightened and which often covered my face with an unexpected flush. At times I even resented and felt ashamed of my childish privileges. At other times I was overcome by a feeling of wonder and I would steal off to some place where I could not be seen, as though wishing to take breath and to remember something—something I seemed to remember very well, but which I had suddenly forgotten and without which I could not show myself for the time being and, indeed, could not exist.

Sometimes I could not help feeling that I was concealing something from everyone, but did not tell anyone about it because, small boy that I was, I was deeply ashamed of it. In the vortex that surrounded me I soon became conscious of a certain feeling of loneliness. There were other children at the country-house, but all were either much older or much younger than I; anyway, I did not feel like having anything to do with them. Of course, nothing would have happened to me if I had not been in an exceptional position. In the eyes of all those beautiful women I was still the small, undefinable creature whom they occasionally liked to caress and with whom they could play as with a little doll. One of them in particular, a ravishing blonde, with very thick, luxuriant hair, whom I had never seen before and shall probably never see again, seemed to have taken a vow never to leave me in peace. I was confused while she was amused by the laughter which she continually aroused all around us by her wild, mad pranks with me, which she seemed to enjoy enormously. Among her schoolfriends at her boarding-school she would certainly have been nicknamed a tom-boy. She was ravishingly beautiful, and there was some-

thing in her beauty which caught one's attention at
the first glance. She certainly bore no resemblance to
the shy, fair-haired little girls who are white as down
and sweet as white mice or clergymen's daughters. She
was not very tall and was a little plump, but had lovely,
delicate, exquisitely cut features. There was something
flashing like lightning in her face, and she was all like
fire, light, swift, alive. Sparks seemed to gleam from
her big, open eyes; they flashed like diamonds, and I
would never exchange such sparkling blue eyes for any
black ones, even if they were blacker than a pair of
Andalusian eyes; indeed, my blonde was a match for
the famous brunette whom a well-known, excellent
poet celebrated in a beautiful poem, in which he vowed
by all Castile that he would gladly break all his bones if
he were allowed to touch the mantilla of his beauty
with the tip of his finger. Add to that, that *my* beauty
was the gayest in all the world, the merriest madcap
creature, playful as a child in spite of the fact that she
had been married for five years. Laughter never left her
lips which were as fresh as the morning rose that has
this minute—with the first ray of sunshine—opened its
fragrant, crimson bud still covered with big, cool
dewdrops.

I remember that the day after my arrival they were
giving a performance of a play. The ballroom was, as
they say, packed to overflowing; there was not a single
vacant seat. As I happened for some reason to be late,
I had to enjoy the performance standing. But the play
was so amusing that I was drawn nearer and nearer to
the stage till I found myself imperceptibly at the front
row where I finally stopped, leaning my elbows on the
back of an armchair on which a young woman was sit-

ting. It was my blond charmer, but we had not yet
been introduced. Without, somehow, being aware of it,
I found myself gazing at her beautifully shaped,
ravishing shoulders, plump and white as foaming milk,
though it did not matter to me in the least whether
I gazed at the lovely shoulders of a woman or at the
bonnet with scarlet ribbons that hid the grey hair of
an old lady in the front row. Next to the blonde sat an
old maid, one of those who, as I happened to observe
later, always took refuge as near as possible to young
and pretty women, choosing preferably those who like
the company of young men. But that is not the point;
only the old maid, having noticed my intent gaze, bent
over to her neighbour and, giggling, whispered something in her ear. The young woman turned round at
once, and I remember that her fiery eyes so flashed
on me in the semi-darkness that, unprepared for the
encounter, I started as though burned. The beauty
smiled.

"Do you like the play?" she asked, looking smilingly
and mockingly at me.

"Yes," I replied, still looking at her in a kind of
amazement, which, in turn, seemed to please her.

"But why are you standing? You'll get tired. Can't
you find a seat?"

"I'm afraid I can't," I replied, this time more preoccupied with my predicament than with the beauty's
sparkling eyes and quite seriously overjoyed to have
found at last a kind heart to whom I could confide my
troubles. "I have looked everywhere," I added, as
though complaining to her that all the seats were
taken, "but all the seats are taken."

"Come here," she said quickly, eager to carry out any

decision as well as any crazy idea that might flash through her scatter-brained head. "Come here, sit on my lap."

"On your lap?" I repeated, taken aback.

I have already mentioned that I had begun to be seriously offended by my privileges and ashamed of them. This one, as though wishing to make fun of me, had gone much farther than the others. Besides, always a shy and timid boy, I had begun to be particularly shy with women and was, therefore, terribly disconcerted now.

"Yes, on my lap," she insisted. "Why, don't you want to sit on my lap?" she asked, beginning to laugh louder and louder, so that in the end she screamed with laughter, goodness knows at what, perhaps at her idea, or perhaps at my confusion. But that was exactly what she wanted.

I blushed and, in my confusion, began to look round for a way of escape. But she guessed my intention and, somehow, managed to catch hold of my hand to make sure that I did not run away, and pulling it towards her, suddenly, quite unexpectedly, and to my utter amazement, squeezed it painfully in her mischievous warm fingers and began to bend my fingers back till they hurt so much that I had to force myself not to cry out and, in doing so, pulled the funniest faces. Moreover, I was terribly surprised, bewildered and even horrified to discover that there were young women so absurd and malicious as to talk such nonsense to boys and pinch them so painfully, goodness only knows for what reason, and before everybody. I expect my unhappy face reflected my utter bewilderment, for the mischievous young woman laughed in

my face, as though she were crazy, and meantime continued to pinch and bend my poor fingers more and
more fiercely. She was highly delighted to have been
successful in playing such a schoolboyish prank and to
confuse and completely mystify a poor boy at the same
time. My position was desperate. In the first place I
was overwhelmed with shame, for everyone near had
turned round to look at us, some in perplexity, others
laughingly, for they realised at once that the beauty
was up to some mischief. Besides, I badly wanted to
scream, for she was bending back my fingers so furiously, as if wishing to punish me for not screaming.
But, like a true Spartan, I made up my mind to endure
the pain, afraid of causing a panic by my screams and
not ever being able to live it down. At last, in utter
despair I began to struggle, trying with all my might
to pull away my hand, but my tormentor was much
stronger than I. At length I could hold out no longer
and uttered a scream—that was what she was waiting
for! Instantly she let go of my hand and turned away
as though nothing had happened, as though it were
not she but someone else who had been up to some
mischief, exactly like a schoolboy, who, as soon as
the master's back is turned, pinches some small, weak
boy near him, or gives him a fillip, a kick, or a push
with his elbow, and immediately turns round again,
puts himself to rights, buries his head in his book and
starts doing his work, in this way making a complete
fool of his infuriated teacher, who had pounced like
a hawk at the noise.

But, fortunately, the general attention was at that
moment fixed on the masterly acting of our host, who

was playing the chief part in some comedy of Scribe's.[1]
Everyone clapped, and, taking advantage of the noise,
I darted from the row of chairs and ran to the opposite
corner of the room from where, skulking behind a
pillar, I looked with horror towards the place where
my treacherous beauty was sitting. She was still laughing, holding her handkerchief to her lips. For a long
time she kept turning round, trying to discover where
I was hiding and, I suppose, feeling very sorry that
our stupid fight had come to an end so soon and
wondering what other prank she could play on me.

That was the beginning of our acquaintance, and
from that evening she never let me alone. She persecuted me without restraint or conscience and became my oppressor and tormentor. The funny part of
her game consisted of pretending to be head over heels
in love with me and teasing me about it in front of
everybody. It goes without saying that to a wild
creature like me it was all so unbearable and vexing
that it almost reduced me to tears, and so serious had
the situation become that I was several times on the
point of having a fight with my treacherous adorer.
My naïve confusion and desperate distress seemed to
inspire her to redouble her persecution. She knew no
pity, while I did not know how to get away from her.
The laughter which arose around us and which she
knew how to provoke merely egged her on to fresh
pranks. But at last people began to find that her jokes
were going a little too far. Indeed, as I remember now,
she did go rather too far with a child like me. But that
was her character. She was a thoroughly spoiled child.

[1] Eugène Scribe (1791–1861), popular French dramatist.

I heard afterwards that it was her husband more than anyone else who spoiled her. He was a very stout, very short and very ruddy-faced man, a very rich and successful businessman, at least he gave that impression: he was always fidgeting and bustling and could not stay two hours in one place. He drove to Moscow every day, sometimes twice a day, and always, as he assured everybody, on some business. It would be difficult to find a more cheerful or more good-humoured face than his comical and yet always honest countenance. He loved his wife not only to the point of feebleness and pitifulness, but he worshipped her like an idol.

He did nothing to restrain her. She had lots of men and women friends. In the first place, very few people did not like her and, secondly, the frivolous creature was herself not particularly discriminating in the choice of her friends, though fundamentally her character was much more serious than might be supposed from what I have just said about her. Of all her friends she preferred and liked best a young married woman, a distant relative of hers, who was also a guest at the country house. There was a kind of tender and refined relationship between them. It was one of those relationships that are sometimes formed by two characters who often are quite the opposite of each other, one of them more austere, deeper, and purer, and the other aware of her friend's superiority, cherishing her friendship as something precious, and submitting to it lovingly with great humility and an honourable sense of her own worth. It is then that this tender and noble refinement in the relationship between these two begins: love and infinite indulgence on one side and

respect and love on the other—respect bordering almost on fear and anxiety about the impression one
makes on the person one values so highly, and on a
jealous and ardent desire to get closer and closer with
every step in life to the heart of that person. Both
friends were of the same age, but there was an im-
measurable difference between them in everything—in
looks, to begin with. Mrs. M—— was also very good-
looking, but there was something special in her beauty,
something that put her apart from the crowd of other
pretty women; there was something in her face that
immediately exerted an irrepressible attraction on
everyone, or rather that aroused a noble and lofty
feeling of sympathy for her in everyone who met her.
There are such fortunate faces. Everyone somehow felt
better, freer, and more cordial beside her, and yet her
big, sad eyes, full of fire and strength, had a timid and
anxious look, as though she were constantly expecting
something hostile and menacing. This strange timidity
sometimes cast such a gloom over her serene, gentle
features, which were so reminiscent of the bright faces
of Italian madonnas, that, looking at her, one soon
grew melancholy, as if it were some sadness of one's
very own. The pale, thin face, in which the clear out-
line of early childhood shone through the perfect
beauty of pure, regular lines, and the despondent
severity of some suppressed, hidden grief—the image
of the trustful years and, perhaps, naïve happiness of
the more recent past, the gentle, but rather timid and
hesitating smile—all this made one feel so unconsciously drawn to that woman that everyone's heart
was filled with a sweet and warm anxiety which spoke
loudly on her behalf even at a distance and made one

feel akin to her even before one got to know her well. But the beautiful woman somehow seemed silent and reserved, although no one could be more attentive and loving to anyone who needed sympathy. There are women who are like sisters of charity in life. One need hide nothing from them, at least no deep-seated affection of the heart and mind. Anyone who is suffering may go to them boldly and hopefully without fear of being a burden, because few of us know how much infinite patience and love, compassion and forgiveness might be found in some woman's heart. Inexhaustible treasures of sympathy, consolation, and hope are to be found in these pure hearts, which are also often hurt, for a heart that loves much grieves much, but its wounds are carefully hidden from inquisitive eyes. For deep sorrow is most often silent and hidden. They are not aghast at the depth of the wound, nor at its suppuration, nor at its stench; anyone who comes to them is by that very fact worthy of them. They seem, indeed, to be born for great, heroic deeds. . . . Mrs. M—— was tall, slender, and graceful, but a little too thin. All her movements somehow seemed uneven, sometimes slow, light, and even dignified, and sometimes childishly quick and, at the same time, there was, in her bearing, a kind of timid humility, something tremulous and defenceless, though it neither prayed for nor asked anyone for protection.

I have mentioned earlier that the reprehensible attentions of the treacherous blonde made me feel ashamed and hurt and stung me to the quick. But there was another strange, secret, and stupid reason for that, a reason which I concealed and which made me shudder as if I had come face to face with the wicked sorcerer Kaschey himself. Skulking, with my head thrown back, alone, in some dark, mysterious corner where the inquisitorial, sardonic look of no blue-eyed rogue could reach me, I nearly died with confusion, shame, and fear at the very thought of it. In short, I was in love. But even assuming that I am talking nonsense, that I could not possibly have been in love, how was it that of all the faces around me only one face caught my attention? Why was it that she was the only one I liked to follow with my eyes, though at that time I certainly cared little for the society of women or sought their acquaintance. It happened mostly in the evenings, when bad weather kept everyone indoors and when, lurking in some corner of the ballroom and unable to find anything else to do, I kept staring aimlessly around me, for, with the exception of my persecutors, people seldom talked to me, and I was terribly bored on such evenings. It was then that I stared at the people round me and listened to their conversation, though often I did not understand a single word of it. It was just at that time that the gentle eyes, the tender smile, and the lovely face of Mrs. M—— (for it was she I was in love with), goodness only knows why, caught my fascinated attention, and this strange, vague, but indescribably sweet sensation was never blotted out from my memory. Often for hours together I seemed to be unable to tear myself away from her. I remembered every gesture, every movement of hers, listened avidly to every vibration of her rich, silvery, but somewhat muffled voice, and—strange to say—the impression that remained with me most of all, apart from the one that was both sweet and timid, was that of an inexplicable curiosity. It looked as if I were on the trail of some mystery.

What I resented most was to be mocked at in the presence of Mrs. M——. I could not help regarding these mocking remarks and waggish persecutions as humiliating. Whenever there happened to be a general burst of laughter at my expense, in which even Mrs. M—— sometimes could not help joining, I would tear myself from my tormentors in sheer despair and, beside myself with grief, run upstairs, where I skulked for the rest of the day, not daring to show my face in the drawing-room. However, I did not as yet understand my shame or my agitation: I went through the whole process unconsciously. So far I had not exchanged two words with Mrs. M——, and, indeed, I dared not do so. One evening, after a most miserable day, I lagged behind the rest during a walk in the country, and, feeling terribly tired, made my way home through the garden. On a seat in a secluded avenue I saw Mrs. M——. She was sitting quite alone, as though she had purposely chosen this secluded spot, her head drooping, and mechanically twisting her handkerchief in her hand. She was lost in thought and did not hear when I came alongside of her.

Noticing me, she quickly rose from her seat and turned away. I saw her quickly wipe her eyes with her handkerchief. She had been crying. Drying her eyes, she gave me a smile and walked back to the house with me. I don't remember what we talked about, but she kept sending me off on one pretext or another, sometimes to pick her a flower and sometimes to see who was riding in the next avenue. Every time I walked away from her, she put her handkerchief to her eyes

again and wiped away the disobedient tears, which refused to leave her and again and again boiled up in
her heart and gushed from her poor eyes. I realised
that I must be very much in her way if she sent me off
so often. Moreover, she was herself aware that I
noticed everything, but she still could not control herself and that made me more and more sorry for her.
I was angry with myself at that moment. I was almost
in despair and cursed myself for my awkwardness and
unresourcefulness. But I still did not know how to
leave her more cannily without showing that I had
noticed her distress. I kept walking beside her in
sorrowful consternation and almost in alarm, not
knowing what to do, and lost for a word to carry on
our scanty conversation.

I was so struck by this meeting that I stealthily kept
Mrs. M—— under observation the whole evening with
avid curiosity and without taking my eyes off her for
a moment. She caught me twice unawares as I was
watching her, and, the second time, noticing me, she
smiled at me. It was the only time she smiled that
evening. The look of sadness never left her face, which
was now very pale. She was talking quietly all the time
to a bad-tempered and cantankerous old lady, whom
nobody liked because of her spying and scandal-
mongering, but of whom everyone was afraid and,
therefore, forced to be nice to whether they liked
it or not.

At ten o'clock Mrs. M——'s husband arrived. Till
that moment I watched her very carefully without
taking my eyes from her sad face; now at the unexpected arrival of her husband I saw her give a violent
start. Her face, already pale, turned suddenly as white

as a sheet. It was so noticeable that the others, too,
saw it. From some scraps of conversation which I over-
heard I gathered that poor Mrs. M—— was far from
happy. It was said that her husband was as jealous as
a blackamoor, not so much from love as from vanity.
He was, above all, a European, a modern man, who on
every possible occasion showed off his belief in the new
ideas. In appearance he was a very tall, dark-haired,
rather thick-set man, with European side-whiskers, a
smug red face, teeth white as sugar, and an irreproachably gentlemanly bearing. He was called a
"clever man." That is the name given in certain circles
to a peculiar species of mankind, men who have grown
fat at other people's expense, who because they do
absolutely nothing and have no intention of doing anything, have a lump of fat instead of a heart as a result
of their perpetual laziness and idleness. These men always tell you that they cannot do anything because of
a concatenation of complicated and hostile circumstances which "paralyse" their "genius" and that was
why people were "sorry" for them. That is the sort of
highfalutin phraseology they use, their *mot d'ordre*,
their slogan and watchword, a phrase which these
well-fed, fat fellows are fond of using every minute
everywhere, a phrase of which people have grown sick
and tired a long time ago as a piece of rank Tartuffism
and as so much fustian. Moreover, some of these amusing fellows who simply cannot find anything to do—
not that they ever try to find it—do their utmost to
make everyone believe that they have not a lump of
fat for a heart, but, on the contrary, something "very
deep," though what exactly it is, not the greatest sur-
geon would have diagnosed, out of politeness, of

course. These gentlemen make their way in the world by concentrating all their instincts on sneering, niggling censure, and boundless arrogance. As they have nothing better to do than to make a note of and memorise the mistakes and weaknesses of other people, and as they have no more good feeling than has fallen to the lot of an oyster, they don't find it difficult with such safeguards to live among people without running into trouble. They are very proud of that. They are, for instance, almost certain that the whole world owes them a living, that the world is theirs, and that they can put it away for future consumption like an oyster; that all but they are fools; that everyone is like an orange or a sponge which they can squeeze dry as soon as they want the juice; that they are masters over everything; and that all this highly commendable order of things is entirely due to the fact that they are such clever men of strong character. In their immense vanity they do not admit any shortcomings in themselves. They are like that species of worldly rogues, born Tartuffes and Falstaffs, who have got themselves so involved in their rogueries they are convinced that that is as it should be, namely, that to live is to carry on swindling people. They have so often assured everyone that they are honest men that in the end they have convinced themselves that they are honest men and that their roguery is honesty. Their conscience does not stretch to self-criticism and generous self-appraisal; they are too fat for some things. Their own precious personality, their Moloch and Baal, their magnificent ego is always in the forefront everywhere. They regard all nature and the whole world as no more than a magnificent mirror which has been created solely to enable the little god to admire himself in it continually and see nothing and no one but himself; it is no wonder, therefore, that to him everything in the world is so hideous a sight. He has a ready phrase for everything and—what is so miraculous and so supremely clever of him—the most fashionable phrase. It is such people, in fact, who help to create fashion by unanimously spreading all over town an idea, which they sense will be successful. Indeed, they have a flair for nosing out such a fashionable phrase which they adopt before everyone else so that it seems as though they have invented it. They are particularly anxious to lay in a good supply of phrases to express their profound sympathy for humanity, to define what is the most correct and rational form of philanthropy and, finally, to decry romanticism or, in other words, the truly beautiful, every atom of which is more precious than all their slimy breed. They are too coarse to recognise truth in an irregular, transitory and unfinished form and they reject everything that is immature, unstable and still in a state of ferment. The well-fed man has spent all his life in a continual round of pleasures, without a worry in the world, without doing anything himself and without knowing how hard work can be. One must, therefore, be very careful not to hurt his fat feelings by any kind of roughness. That he will never forgive you. He will always remember it and take pleasure in avenging it. To sum up: my hero is neither more nor less than a huge, blown-up bag, stuffed with maxims, fashionable phrases, and all sorts of labels.

Mr. M——, however, had a special talent of his own and was in a way quite a remarkable man: he was a wit, a good talker, and *raconteur*, and there was always a crowd of people round him in drawing-rooms. That evening he was particularly successful in creating an impression. He took possession of the conversation; he was in good form, gay, pleased with himself, and did succeed in drawing everyone's attention to himself. But Mrs. M—— looked ill all the time; her face was so sad that it seemed to me that any moment tears would begin to tremble on her long eyelashes. All this, as I have said, surprised and astonished me greatly. I went to bed with a feeling of a strange kind of curiosity and all night I dreamed of Mr. M——, though till then I had seldom had bad dreams.

Early next morning I was summoned to a rehearsal of some tableaux vivants in which I had a part. There were to be tableaux vivants, a play, then a dance—all in one evening—five days later in celebration of the birthday of our host's youngest daughter. Another hundred guests from Moscow and the neighbouring country houses were invited to this almost improvised entertainment, so that there was a great deal of fuss, bustle, and commotion. The rehearsal, or rather the fitting of the costumes, was not fixed at the usual time, but early in the morning, because our producer, the well-known artist R——, a friend of our host's, who agreed to devise and produce the tableaux vivants as well as to train us, was in a hurry to leave for Moscow to purchase the props and to make the final preparations for the birthday party. There was, therefore, no time to lose. I took part in one tableau with Mrs M——, a scene from mediaeval life which was called: "The Lady of the Castle and her Page."

On meeting Mrs. M—— at the rehearsal, I was overcome by an inexplicable feeling of confusion. I could not help feeling that she would immediately read in my eyes the thoughts, doubts, and conjectures that had arisen in my mind since the previous day. I felt, besides, that in a way I was to blame for having found her in tears the day before and had interrupted her grief so that she had involuntarily to look at me askance as an unwelcome witness and an uninvited participant of her secret. But, thank God, the rehearsal went off without any trouble: I was simply not noticed. She seemed to pay no attention to me or to the rehearsal: she was absent-minded, sad, and gloomily pensive. It was clear that she was greatly worried by something. As soon as my part was over, I ran off to change my clothes and ten minutes later came out onto the terrace leading into the garden. Mrs. M—— came out of another door almost at the same time and at that very moment her self-satisfied husband appeared from the opposite direction. He was returning from the garden, after escorting a large group of ladies and handing them over to an agreeable *cavaliere-servente*. The meeting of husband and wife was apparently quite unexpected. Mrs. M—— for some unknown reason was suddenly covered with confusion and betrayed her feeling of slight vexation by an impatient movement. The husband, who had been whistling some aria, quite unconcerned, and thoughtfully stroking his side-whiskers on the way to the terrace, frowned on meeting his wife, examining her, as I remember now, with a decidedly inquisitorial gaze.

"Going into the garden?" he asked, noticing the parasol and book in his wife's hand.

"No," she replied, blushing a little, "to the wood."

"By yourself?"

"With him," Mrs. M—— said, pointing at me. "I usually go for walks alone in the morning," she added in a faltering, uncertain voice, the sort of voice in which one tells a lie for the first time.

"I see. . . . I've just escorted a whole party there. They are all gathering there in the flower arbour to see N—— off. He's going away, you know. . . . There's been some trouble in his family in Odessa. . . . Your cousin," he went on, referring to the blond charmer, "is laughing and crying at the same time. I can't make her out. She did tell me, though, that you're cross with N—— for some reason, and that's why you didn't go to see him off. It's nonsense, of course, isn't it?"

"She's not serious," replied Mrs. M——, coming down the steps of the terrace.

"So this is your daily *cavaliere-servente*," said Mr. M——, looking at me through his lorgnette.

"Page!" I cried, angered by the lorgnette and his sarcastic tone and, laughing straight in his face, I jumped down the three steps of the terrace at one bound.

"A pleasant walk," murmured Mr. M—— and went on his way.

Of course, I had gone up to Mrs. M—— the moment she pointed me out to her husband, pretending that she had invited me to do so an hour before and that I had accompanied her on her walks every morning for the last month. But I could not make out why she had been so confused, why she had looked so embarrassed and what she had in mind when she decided to take refuge in her little lie. Why had she not simply said that she was going for a walk alone? Now I dared not even look at her, but, my curiosity getting the better of me, I began surreptitiously to steal a look at her face in a most naïve way; but just as an hour before at the rehearsal, she did not notice my surreptitious looks nor my mute questions. The same tormenting anxiety, but more clearly and more intensely, was now reflected in her face, in her agitated state, in her walk. She was in a hurry to go somewhere, quickening her steps more and more and glancing uneasily down every avenue, every clearing in the wood that led in the direction of the garden. I, too, was waiting for something to happen. Suddenly we heard the sound of horses' hoofs behind us. It was the cavalcade of ladies and gentlemen who were seeing off N——, who was so suddenly leaving our company.

Among the ladies was my blond charmer, whom Mr. M—— had mentioned when he told us about her tears. But she was, as usual, laughing loudly like a child as she galloped briskly on her beautiful bay horse. On coming up to us, N—— took off his hat, but he did not stop, nor say one word to Mrs. M——. Soon the whole crowd disappeared from our sight. I glanced at Mrs. M—— and almost cried out in amazement: she was standing as white as a sheet and big tears were rolling down her cheeks. Our eyes met accidentally: Mrs. M—— suddenly blushed, turned away for a moment, and an unmistakable look of uneasiness and vexation flitted across her face. I was not wanted, it was much worse than the day before—that was as clear as daylight, but where was I to go?

Suddenly, guessing what I felt, Mrs. M—— opened the book, which she had in her hand, and, reddening and obviously trying not to look at me, said, as though she had only at that moment realised it:

"Goodness, this is the second part. I've made a mistake. Please, bring me the first."

It was impossible to misunderstand her: my part was over, and I could not have been told to make myself scarce more clearly.

I ran off with the book and did not come back. The first part remained lying quite undisturbed on the table that morning.

But I was not myself: my heart throbbed as though in perpetual alarm. I did my best to avoid a meeting with Mrs. M——. But I looked with a kind of wild curiosity at the smug figure of Mr. M——, as though there ought to be something special about him now. I simply cannot understand the cause of that absurd curiosity of mine. All I can remember is that I was in a strange state of bewilderment at what I had happened to see that morning. But my day was only just beginning and it was chock-full of incidents for me.

Dinner seemed very early that day. In the evening we were all supposed to go on a trip to a village fête in the neighbourhood and we all had to be ready on time. I had been dreaming of this fête for the last three days, expecting to enjoy myself hugely. Almost all the party gathered for coffee on the terrace. I followed the others cautiously and concealed myself behind the three rows of chairs. I was drawn there by curiosity and yet the last thing I wanted was to be seen by Mrs. M——. But, as ill luck would have it, I found myself not far from my blond tormentor. This time a miracle, something that seemed impossible, had come to pass: she looked twice as beautiful. I don't know how and why it all happens, but with women such miracles are not at all rare. This time we had a new visitor: a tall, pale-faced young man, an inveterate admirer of our blond charmer, who had just arrived from Moscow as though for the sole purpose of taking the place of N——, who was rumoured to be head over heels in love with her. As for the newcomer, he had for a long time been on the same terms with her as Benedick with Beatrice in Shakespeare's *Much Ado About Nothing*. In short, our charmer was enjoying an immense success that day. Her jokes and chatter were so full of grace, so trustfully naïve, so excusably imprudent; she was convinced of universal adoration with such graceful self-confidence that she really was, as it were, the cynosure of all eyes. She was constantly surrounded by a close circle of surprised and admiring listeners, and she had never been so ravishing. Every word she uttered struck her audience as wonderful and seductive, was caught up and spread around, and not a single jest, not a single sally of hers was lost. Indeed, no one seemed to have expected such taste, such brilliance, such intelligence from her. All her best qualities were daily buried under the most wilful and extravagant behaviour, the most obstinate, schoolgirlish pranks, almost verging on buffoonery, and were rarely noticed, and, when noticed, hardly ever believed in, so that now her extraordinary success was met by a general eager whisper of amazement.

However, a rather delicate and peculiar circumstance contributed to her success, at least judging by the part played in it by Mrs. M——'s husband. The mischievous rogue made up her mind—and, it must be added, to the delight of almost everyone and certainly to the satisfaction of the young people—to launch a fierce attack on Mr. M—— for reasons which she ap-

parently considered important. She, therefore, engaged in a veritable battle of witticisms, gibes, and
sarcastic innuendoes of the most irresistible, elusive,
treacherous, smooth, and hidden kind, which inexorably hit home without giving her victim any chance of
retaliation, but only exhausted him in fruitless efforts
and reduced him to fury and comic despair.

I don't know for certain, but I believe this attack
was premeditated and not improvised. This desperate
duel had begun at dinner. I say "desperate" because
Mr. M—— did not give in for a long time. He had to
summon all his presence of mind, all his wit, all his
rare resourcefulness not to be routed, decisively beaten,
and covered completely with ignominy. The verbal en-
gagement was accompanied by the continuous and irrepressible laughter of all those who were present and
took part in it. This day, at any rate, was quite different for him from the day before. It was noticeable
several times that Mrs. M—— was anxious to stop her
incautious friend, who, in turn, seemed to be absolutely determined to array the jealous husband in the
most absurd jester's costume as well as, I suppose, in
the costume of Bluebeard. At least that much I remember, and this is confirmed by the part I myself
was to play in this head-on collision.

It all happened suddenly, in a most absurd manner,
and quite unexpectedly. At that moment I was standing where everybody could see me, without suspecting
any evil and even forgetting to take the precautions I
had taken not so long ago. I found myself suddenly
pushed to the forefront as the mortal enemy and natural rival of Mr. M——, as one who was desperately
and hopelessly in love with his wife. My tormentor

swore that she was telling the truth and said that she could prove it, for only that morning she had seen in the wood . . .

But I did not give her time to finish. I interrupted her at the most desperate moment of my life. That moment was so shamelessly calculated, was so treacherously prepared to lead up to its conclusion, to its ridiculous *dénouement*, and fitted out with such side-splitting fun that this last sally was greeted with an explosion of universal and uncontrollable laughter. And though I immediately guessed that mine was not the most vexatious part in the performance, I was so overcome with confusion, so irritated and startled, that, in tears, and full of misery and despair and breathless with shame, I tore through two rows of chairs, stepped forward and, addressing my tormentor, cried in a voice choked with tears and indignation:

"Aren't you ashamed . . . aloud . . . before all the ladies . . . to—to tell such a wicked lie? You're just like a small child . . . before all these men. . . . What will they say? You—a grown-up married woman . . ."

But before I had time to finish there was a deafening roar of applause. My protest created a perfect *furor*. My naïve gesture, my age, but, above all, the fact that I seemed to take Mr. M——'s part—all this provoked such an outburst of infernal laughter that even today I cannot help feeling terribly amused at the mere recollection of it. I was struck dumb and almost senseless with horror. I buried my burning face in my hands and rushed out of the drawing-room, knocking a tray out of the hands of a footman who was just coming in, and flew upstairs to my room. I pulled out the key outside the door and locked myself in. I did well, for there was a hue and cry after me. In less than a minute my door was besieged by a crowd of the prettiest young women. I could hear their ringing laughter, their rapid chatter, and their merry voices; they were twittering all at once like swallows. All of them, every one of them, begged and besought me to open the door for only one minute; they swore that they meant not the least harm to me, that all they wanted was to smother me with kisses. But—what could be more terrible than this new threat? I was burning with shame behind the door of my room, my face buried in the pillows. I did not open the door. I did not even respond. They kept knocking and beseeching me for a long time, but I was insensible and deaf, like a boy of eleven.

Well, what was I to do now? Everything was discovered, everything I had so jealously guarded and concealed had been laid bare. . . . I should be exposed to everlasting shame and disgrace. To tell the truth, I did not know myself what I was so afraid of and what it was that I wished to conceal; but I was all the same frightened of something, and for the discovery of this "something" I trembled like a leaf. One thing I had not known till that minute was what it was: whether it was good or bad, glorious or disgraceful, praiseworthy or unpraiseworthy. Now, however, in my agony and enforced anguish, I realised that it was *ridiculous* and *shameful*. At the same time I felt instinctively that such a verdict was false, inhuman, and coarse; but I was crushed, annihilated; the process of conscious thought seemed to have stopped in me and thrown me into confusion; I could neither oppose that verdict nor consider it properly. All I was conscious of was that my heart had been inhumanly and shamelessly wounded and I dissolved in impotent tears. I was exasperated. I was boiling over with indignation and hatred, which I had never known before. For it was the first time in my life that I had experienced real grief, insult, and injury; and it was all really true, without any exaggeration. The first still inexperienced and unformed feeling had been rudely disturbed in me, a mere child; the first fragrant, virginal feeling of shame had been so early exposed and desecrated, and the first and, perhaps, very serious, aesthetic impression had been held up to scorn. Of course, the people who had scoffed at me did not know a great deal about my sufferings and they could not have any inkling of them. One secret circumstance which I had no time and was afraid to analyse was also partly responsible for my state of mind. I went on lying on my bed in anguish and despair, my face buried in my pillows, hot and shivery in turn. Two questions worried me: what had that odious blonde seen, what could she have seen today in the wood between Mrs. M—— and me? And, secondly, how could I look Mrs. M—— in the face and not die on the spot at that very moment of shame and despair.

An unusual noise in the courtyard at last aroused me from the state of semi-consciousness into which I had fallen. I got up and went up to the window. The whole courtyard was crowded with carriages, saddle-horses, and bustling servants. They were apparently about to leave; a few riders had already mounted their horses; other guests were taking their seats in the carriages. It was then that I remembered the trip to the village fête, and gradually a feeling of uneasiness stole into my heart. I began looking intently for my German pony in the yard. There was no pony there, so they must have forgotten me. I could no longer restrain myself and rushed headlong downstairs without thinking of any unpleasant meetings or of my recent disgrace.

Terrible news awaited me. This time there was neither a horse for me nor a place in any of the carriages. Everything had been taken and distributed, and I was forced to give place to others.

Completely taken aback by this new blow, I remained standing on the steps of the terrace and gazed mournfully at the long row of coaches, cabriolets, and carriages in which there was not even a little corner for me, and at the smartly dressed horsewomen, under whom their restless horses were prancing.

One of the riders was late for some reason. They were only waiting for his arrival before setting off. His horse was standing at the entrance, champing the bit, pawing the ground with its hoofs, and shuddering and rearing every moment. Two stable-boys were cautiously holding it by the bridle and everyone else was standing apprehensively at a respectful distance from it.

A most unfortunate circumstance had occurred which prevented me from going. Apart from the arrival of new visitors who had taken all the seats and all the horses, two of the horses had fallen ill, including my German pony. But I was not the only one to suffer because of it: it appeared that there was no horse for our new visitor, the pale-faced young man I have mentioned earlier. To avoid any discourtesy, our host was forced to resort to the extreme step of recom-

mending his fierce, unbroken stallion, adding, to salve
his conscience, that it was quite impossible to ride it
and that he had long decided to sell it because of its
vicious character, if only a purchaser could be found.
Though forewarned, the visitor declared that he
wasn't a bad horseman and that he was ready to mount
any horse rather than not go. Our host said nothing
at the time, but I could not help noticing that a sly
and somewhat ambiguous smile hovered over his lips.
While waiting for the young man who had been so
sure of his horsemanship, our host did not mount his
horse, but kept rubbing his hands impatiently and
continually glancing at the door. Something of the
kind communicated itself also to the two stable-boys
who were holding the stallion and were almost breathless with pride at seeing themselves before the whole
company in charge of a horse that might any minute
kill a man for no reason at all. Something similar to
their master's sly smile was also reflected in their eyes,
bulging with expectation and fixed on the door from
which the daredevil visitor was to appear. Finally, the
horse, too, behaved as though it had come to an un-
derstanding with our host and the stable-boys: it carried itself proudly and haughtily, as though feeling
that it was being watched by several dozen curious
eyes and as though showing off before them all, proud
of its disgraceful reputation exactly as some incorrigi-
ble scapegrace is proud of his criminal exploits. It
seemed to be challenging any daredevil who would
presume to curb its independence.

The daredevil made his appearance at last. Somewhat abashed at having kept everyone waiting and
hurriedly pulling on his gloves, he came forward with-

out looking, went down the steps, and only raised his eyes as he stretched out his hand to grasp the withers of the waiting horse. But he was suddenly startled by its furious rearing and the warning cry from all the frightened spectators. The young man stepped back and looked bewildered at the savage horse which was quivering all over, snorting with fury, and wildly rolling its bloodshot eyes, continually sinking back on its hind legs and rearing its forelegs as though about to dart off into the air and carry the two stable-boys with it. For a moment the young man stood completely perplexed, then blushing slightly with some embarrassment, raised his eyes, looked round him, and gazed at the frightened women.

"A very fine horse," he said, as though to himself, "and, from what I can see of him, it must be a pleasure to ride him, but—but you know what? I don't think I will," he concluded, turning to our host with his good-humoured, broad smile which so suited his kind and intelligent face.

"All the same I consider you an excellent horseman, I swear I do," replied the delighted owner of the unmanageable horse, pressing warmly and even gratefully his guest's hand, "just because you realised from the first moment the sort of brute you had to deal with," he added with dignity. "Would you believe me if I told you that I, who have served twenty-three years in a hussar regiment, have had the pleasure of lying on the ground three times thanks to him, exactly as many times as I have mounted this . . . greedy parasite. Tancred, my friend, there's no one worthy of you here. Your rider, I daresay, must be some legendary Ilya Muromets, who is probably sitting idly in his village of Karachovo now waiting for your teeth to fall out. Come, take him away. It's time he stopped frightening people. It was a waste bringing him out," he concluded, rubbing his hands complacently.

Tancred, it should be observed, was of no use whatsoever to our host, for he just ate his corn and did nothing in return; moreover, the old hussar had lost his reputation as an expert on horses by paying a fabulous sum for the worthless parasite, whose only merit was his beauty. But he was all the same delighted that his Tancred had not lost his dignity, had practically dismounted another horseman, and, therefore, had won for himself new, senseless laurels.

"You're not riding?" cried the blonde, who was quite determined that her *cavaliere-servente* should this time be at her side. "You're not afraid, are you?"

"I am indeed!" replied the young man.

"You're not serious?"

"Look here, you don't want me to break my neck, do you?"

"Then make haste and mount my horse. Don't be afraid, it's very gentle. We won't delay them. They'll change the saddle in a minute. I'll try my luck on your horse. I don't believe Tancred will always be uncivil."

No sooner said than done. The mischievous creature jumped out from the saddle and uttered the last sentence standing before us.

"You don't know Tancred very well if you think he'll allow your silly side-saddle to be put on him, and, besides, I'm damned if I'll let you break your neck, for that would be a pity!" said our host, affecting, at that moment of inward satisfaction, as he always did, a studied brusqueness and even coarseness of speech, which in his opinion went so well with a good fellow, an old soldier, and which he considered would particularly please the ladies. That was one of his delusions, a favourite whim of his with which we were all familiar.

"Well, crybaby, wouldn't you like to have a try? You did want to go, didn't you?" said the valiant horsewoman, noticing me. She pointed teasingly at Tancred, for she did not want to withdraw without some show of heroics, having had to dismount from her horse for nothing and not wanting to leave me without some biting remark, since I had been so unfortunate as to turn up at that moment.

"I don't suppose you're like . . . well," she added, "I mean we all know you're a famous hero and you'd be ashamed to be a coward, wouldn't you, especially," she threw a quick glance at Mrs. M——, whose carriage was nearest to the steps, "when someone is looking at you, you beautiful page."

My heart overflowed with hatred and a wish to get my own back when the fair amazon had come up to us with the intention of mounting Tancred. . . . But I can't describe what I felt at this unexpected challenge by the mischievous creature. Everything seemed to go dark before my eyes when I caught her glance at Mrs. M——. A sudden idea flashed through my mind. . . . But it was only a second, a fraction of a second, it was like a flash of gunpowder! Possibly, too, the cup was full to the brim, and I was suddenly so infuriated that my spirits rose and I felt like destroying all my enemies on the spot and revenging myself on them for everything and in the presence of everybody by showing them what sort of fellow I was. Or, perhaps, by

some miracle I had been taught in an instant mediaeval
history, of which I had known nothing till then, and
tournaments, paladins, heroes, beautiful ladies, glory
and conquerors flashed through my whirling mind: I
could hear the trumpets of heralds, the clanking of
swords, the shouts and applause of the crowd, and
amidst all those shouts one timid cry of a frightened
heart which enchants the proud soul more sweetly
than victories and fame. . . . I'm afraid I don't know
whether all that nonsense had come into my head at
that moment, or whether, more rationally, it was a
presentiment of the inevitable nonsense of the days
to come, only I felt that my hour had struck. My
heart leaped and shuddered, and I don't remember
how I jumped down the steps at one bound and was
beside Tancred.

"You think I'm afraid?" I cried boldly and proudly,
hardly able to see anything in my feverish state,
breathless with excitement and flushing till my tears
scalded my cheeks. "You'll see!" And grasping Tancred's withers, I put my foot in the stirrup before anyone had the time to make the slightest movement. At
that moment Tancred reared, flung up its head and
with one mighty leap tore itself out of the hands of
the startled stable-boys and flew, like a whirlwind, so
that everyone just gasped and uttered a horrified cry.

Goodness only knows how I managed to get my
other leg over the horse while it galloped off at a ter-
rific speed, nor can I imagine how I did not lose the
reins. Tancred carried me beyond the trellis gates,
turned sharply to the right, and galloped off beside
the fence without bothering where he went. It was
only at that instant that I heard a shout from fifty

voices behind me, and that shout was echoed in my sinking heart with such a feeling of satisfaction and pride that I shall never forget that crazy moment of my childhood. All the blood rushed to my head, deafened and overwhelmed me, mastering my fear. I was beside myself. Indeed, recalling it now, I can't help feeling that there was something truly chivalrous about it all.

However, all my chivalry began and was over in less than a moment, or it would have gone badly with the knight. Even then I don't know how I was saved. I knew how to ride: I had had lessons. But my German pony was more like a sheep than a riding horse. Of course, I should have fallen off Tancred, if he had had time to throw me; but after galloping fifty paces, he suddenly took fright at a huge stone which lay beside the road and shied. He turned round so sharply without diminishing his speed that I am still puzzled how I managed not to be flung like a ball twenty feet out of the saddle and be dashed to pieces, or how Tancred did not dislocate his legs by such a sharp turn. He rushed back to the gates, tossing his head furiously, bounding from side to side, as though drunk with rage, flinging his legs helter-skelter in the air, and shaking me off his back at every leap just as if a tiger had jumped onto him and buried its teeth and claws into the horse's flesh. In another moment I should have fallen off. I was already falling, but several riders flew to my rescue. Two of them cut off the way into the open country, two others galloped up so near that they almost crushed my legs when they converged on Tancred from both sides, and both were already hold-

ing him by the bridle. A few seconds later we were at
the steps.

I was taken off the horse, pale and scarcely breath-
ing. I was shaking like a blade of grass in the wind
just like Tancred who was standing motionless and
leaning backwards with his whole body, looking as if
his hoofs were dug into the ground, shaking like a leaf,
his whole body quivering, gasping, and emitting fiery
breath out of his red steaming nostrils, as though
stunned with fury and outraged at the unpunished im-
pudence of a child. Cries of nervousness, surprise, and
panic could be heard all around me.

At that moment my wandering eyes caught the
eyes of Mrs. M——, who looked pale and distressed and
—I shall never forget that moment—instantly the
blood rushed to my face, which glowed and burned
like fire; I don't know what happened to me, but, confused and frightened by my own feelings, I dropped
my eyes timidly. But my glance was noticed, caught,
and stolen from me. All eyes turned on Mrs. M——
and, caught unawares by the general curiosity, she
blushed like a child from some uncontrollable and
naïve feeling and tried her utmost, though rather un-
successfully, to suppress her blush by laughing.

All this, of course, was absurd when looked at from
outside; but at that moment a most unexpected and
naïve escapade saved me from being the object of general laughter by giving a special colour to the whole
adventure. The person responsible for the whole commotion, my fair tormentor, suddenly rushed up to
embrace and kiss me. She had looked at me, hardly
able to believe her eyes, when I dared to accept her
challenge and pick up the gauntlet she had flung at

me when glancing at Mrs. M——. She had nearly died
of fright and remorse when I had flown off on Tancred; but now, when it was all over, and particularly
when, with the others, she caught my glance at Mrs.
M—— and saw my confusion and my sudden flush of
colour, when, finally, because of the romantic turn of
her frivolous mind, she succeeded in giving that moment a kind of new, hidden, and unspoken significance—now, after all that, she was so delighted with
my "chivalry" that she rushed up to me, pressed me
to her bosom, deeply moved, proud of me, and overjoyed. A minute later she raised the most naïve, most
severe little face, on which two little crystal tears
gleamed, and looking at the people who crowded
round us, said in a serious and grave voice, which no
one had ever heard her use before, pointing at me:
"Mais c'est très sérieux, messieurs, ne riez pas!" She
did not seem to be aware that they were all standing in front of her, as though enchanted, gazing in
admiration at her radiant enthusiasm. All this swift,
unexpected action of hers, her serious little face, the
ingenuous *naïveté*, the heartfelt tears no one suspected she was capable of that had started to her per-
petually laughing eyes were such an unlooked-for surprise that they all stood before her as though
electrified by her look, her rapid, fiery words and gestures. It seemed as though they could not take their
eyes off her, afraid to miss that rare moment in her
inspired face. Even our host turned red like a tulip,
and I am assured that he was heard afterwards con-
fessing "to his shame" that he had been in love for a
whole minute with his lovely visitor. It is, of course,
obvious that after this I was a knight, a hero.

"De Lorge! Toggenborg!" I heard them exclaiming all around me.

There was a burst of applause.

"Three cheers for the younger generation!" added our host.

"But he must come, he must come with us!" cried the beauty. "We shall find, we must find a place for him. He shall sit beside me, on my lap. . . . No, no, I'm sorry," she corrected herself, bursting into loud laughter, which she was unable to restrain as she recalled our first encounter. But while laughing, she stroked my hand, trying her utmost to be very nice to me to make sure that I did not take offence.

"Of course, of course!" several voices cried in agreement. "He must come, he has won his place!"

The matter was at once settled. The old maid who had been the cause of my acquaintance with the blond beauty was immediately besieged with requests from all the young people to stay at home and give up her seat to me. She was forced to consent to her intense vexation, smiling and secretly fuming with rage. Her protectress, near whom she was always to be found, my former enemy, and my most recent friend, shouted, as she galloped past her on her mettlesome horse, laughing like a child, that she envied her and would have been glad to stay with her, for it was going to rain and they would all get soaked.

Her prophecy proved all too true. An hour later the rain came pouring down, and our excursion was ruined. We had to wait for the rain to stop for several hours in the cottages of the village and returned home at ten o'clock in the damp weather that followed the rain. I began to be a little feverish. At the moment when we were about to resume our seats in the carriages, Mrs. M—— came up to me and expressed surprise that all I had on was a jacket and that my neck was uncovered. I replied that I had not had time to get my cloak. She took out a pin and pinned up the frilly collar of my shirt, removed from her neck a crimson gauze kerchief and put it round my neck that I might not get a sore throat. She was in such a hurry that I had no time to thank her.

But when we got home, I found her in the little drawing-room with the blond charmer and the pale-faced young man who had distinguished himself today by refusing to ride Tancred. I went up to thank her and return her kerchief. But now, after all my adventures, I felt somehow let down; I would have liked to hurry upstairs and there, at leisure, think it all over. I was so full of all sorts of impressions. As I returned the kerchief, I blushed to my ears as usual.

"I bet he would have liked to keep the kerchief," said the young man, laughing. "I can see that he is sorry to part with it."

"Yes, yes, that is so," the blonde cried. "Good heavens, what a boy!" she said with undisguised vexation, shaking her head, but she stopped in time at a serious glance from Mrs. M——, who did not want to carry the jest too far.

I went away as quickly as possible.

"Goodness, what a silly boy you are!" said the mischievous creature, overtaking me in the next room and taking hold of both my hands amicably. "You needn't have returned the kerchief if you wanted so much to have it. You could have said you mislaid it, and that would have been the end of it. You are a silly boy!

You didn't know how to do so simple a thing! You are funny!"

And she chucked me under the chin, laughing at my having blushed as red as a poppy.

"I'm your friend now, don't you see? Our hostilities are at an end—yes or no?"

I laughed and pressed her fingers in silence.

"I'm glad you agree! Why are you so pale and shivering? Are you feverish?"

"Yes, I don't feel well."

"You poor boy! That's because of all that excitement. Look here, you'd better go to bed without waiting for supper. You'll be all right in the morning. Come along!"

She took me upstairs, and there seemed no end to her solicitude for me. Leaving me to undress, she ran downstairs, got me some tea, and brought it up herself when I was in bed. She also brought me a warm blanket. Surprised and touched by all the care and solicitude for me, or perhaps even more as a result of the events of the whole day, the excursion, and the fever, I embraced her warmly as if she were my closest and dearest friend as I said good night to her. All the impressions of that day rushed to my weakened heart, and I nestled up to her bosom and almost burst into tears. She noticed how deeply moved I was and, I believe, my tomboy was a little moved herself.

"You're a very good boy," she whispered, looking at me with gentle eyes. "Please, don't ever be cross with me. You won't, will you?"

In short, we became the most affectionate and truest friends.

It was rather early when I woke up, but my room

was flooded with sunshine. I jumped out of bed feeling perfectly well and in excellent spirits, as though I had had no fever the night before. Instead, I now felt unutterably happy. I remembered last night's scene and I felt that I would have given anything in the world if I could have embraced my new friend, our fair-haired beauty, at that moment. But it was very early, and everyone was still asleep. I dressed hurriedly, went down into the garden, and from there into the wood. I made my way where the trees were densest and their fragrance more resinous and where the rays of the sun peeped in more gaily, rejoicing that it succeeded here and there in penetrating the dark shadows of the dense foliage. It was a lovely morning.

Imperceptibly working my way further and further, I found myself at the other end of the wood not far from the bank of the river Moskva. It flowed at the bottom of a hill about two hundred yards in front of me. On the opposite bank they were haymaking. I watched the long rows of sharp scythes gleaming all together at every sweeping movement of the haymakers and then suddenly disappearing like fiery snakes, just as if they were hiding somewhere, and the grass, cut at the root, flying on one side in dense, thick piles and laid in long, straight furrows. I don't remember how long I spent in contemplation, when all of a sudden I was aroused by the snorting of a horse that was pawing the ground impatiently about twenty paces from me on a wide clearing that led from the high road to the country house. I don't know whether I heard the horse as soon as the rider rode up and halted, or whether I had been aware of the sound a long time, but that it had fallen on my ear without making any impression and unable to rouse me from my reverie. Curious, I went back into the wood and, having only gone a few yards, I heard voices talking rapidly, but softly. I went up a little closer, carefully parting the branches of the last bushes bordering on the clearing, and immediately sprang back in amazement: a familiar white dress flashed across my eyes, and a woman's soft voice resounded like music in my heart. It was Mrs. M——. She was standing beside the man on horseback, who was hurriedly talking to her. To my surprise, I recognised him as Mr. N——, the young man who had gone away the previous morning and about whom Mr. M—— was so concerned. But at the time it was said that he was going far away, somewhere to the south of Russia, and that was why I was so surprised to see him again at our place so early and alone with Mrs. M——.

She was animated and excited, as I had never seen her before, and tears were glistening on her cheeks. The young man was holding her hand and was kissing it, bending down from the saddle. I had come upon them at the moment of parting. They seemed to be in a hurry. At last he took a sealed envelope out of his pocket, handed it to her, embraced her with one hand as before, and, without dismounting, gave her a long and ardent kiss. A moment later he struck his horse and flashed past me like an arrow. Mrs. M—— followed him with her eyes for a few seconds, then walked back to the house, looking sad and pensive. But after going a few steps along the clearing, she seemed suddenly to recover herself and, hurriedly parting the bushes, walked away through the wood.

I followed her, surprised and perturbed by all that

I had seen. My heart was beating violently, as though from fright. I felt benumbed and perplexed, my thoughts were disjointed and scattered, but I remember that for some reason I felt terribly sad. Now and then I caught a glimpse of her white dress through the foliage. I followed her mechanically, without losing sight of her, but terrified that she might notice me. At last she came out onto the path that led to the garden. After half a minute I, too, came out. Imagine my amazement when I suddenly noticed on the red sand of the path a sealed envelope, which I recognised at the first glance: it was the envelope Mr. N—— had given to Mrs. M—— ten minutes earlier.

I picked it up. The white paper was blank on both sides: there was no inscription on it. It was not large, but it was heavy and bulging, as though there were three or more sheets of notepaper in it. What was the meaning of the envelope? No doubt, it would explain the whole of this mystery. Perhaps in it Mr. N—— told Mrs. M—— all that he had no time to tell her during their brief, hurried rendezvous. He had not even dismounted. . . . Had he been in a hurry, or had he, perhaps, been afraid of not being able to stick to his decision to go away at the hour of parting—goodness knows. . . .

I stopped and without coming out on the path, threw the envelope back in the most conspicuous place. I did not take my eyes off it, thinking that Mrs. M—— would discover the loss and come back to look for it. But after waiting about four minutes, I could not restrain myself, picked up my find again, put it in my pocket and went in pursuit of Mrs. M——. I overtook her in the garden, in the big avenue. She was

going straight to the house, with a quick and hurried
step, but lost in thought, her eyes fixed on the ground.
I did not know what to do. Go up and hand it to her?
That meant that I knew it all and had seen it all. I
would have betrayed myself at the first word. And how
would I look at her? How would she look at me? I kept
expecting that she would recollect herself, discover her
loss and retrace her steps. Then I could, unnoticed,
throw the envelope on the path and she would have
found it. But no! We were already approaching the
house; she had already been seen. . . .

As ill-luck would have it, everyone got up very early
that morning for, after the unsuccessful excursion,
they had arranged a new one the night before. I knew
nothing about it. They were all preparing to start at
once and were having breakfast on the terrace. I lin-
gered for ten minutes, not wishing to be seen with
Mrs. M——. Then, going round the garden, I approached the house from a different direction some-
time after her. She was walking up and down the terrace, looking pale and worried, with her arms folded,
and clearly trying to keep calm and gather enough
strength to suppress the agonising and desperate anguish that could be seen in her eyes, her walk, her
every movement. Occasionally she would go down the
steps and walk a few paces between the flower beds in
the direction of the garden, her eyes eagerly, impatiently, even incautiously looking for something in the
sand of the paths and on the floor of the terrace.
There could be no doubt that she had discovered her
loss and apparently thought that she had dropped the
envelope somewhere near the house—yes, that was so,
she was sure of it!

Someone, followed by others, observed that she was pale and worried. She was overwhelmed with questions about her health and vexatious expressions of sympathy. She had to dismiss their questions with a joke; she had to laugh, to look cheerful. From time to time she looked at her husband, who was standing at the end of the terrace talking to two women, and, as on the first evening of his arrival, the poor woman was seized by the same kind of attack of shivering, the same confusion. Thrusting my hand into my pocket and holding the letter tightly in it, I stood at some distance from all of them, imploring fate that Mrs. M—— should notice me. I wanted to calm her, to cheer her up if only by a glance, to say something surreptitiously to her. But when she did look at me accidentally, I gave a start and dropped my eyes.

I saw how she suffered and I was not mistaken. To this day I don't know her secret, I know nothing except what I saw myself and what I have just described. Their liaison was not perhaps such as one might suppose at the first glance. That kiss was perhaps a farewell kiss, a last, small reward for the sacrifice made to her peace of mind and honour. Mr. N—— was going away, he was leaving her perhaps forever. Finally, even the letter I was holding in my hand—who knows what it contained? How is one to judge? Who is there to condemn? And yet there can be no doubt that a sudden disclosure of her secret would have been a terrible, a crushing blow. I still remember her face at that moment: it was impossible to suffer more. To feel, to know, to be certain, to wait as though for the hour of one's execution, that in a quarter of an hour, in another minute, everything might be discovered, the let-

ter found by someone, picked up; there was no inscription on it, it could be opened, and then—what
then? What punishment could be worse than that
which awaited her? She was walking among those who
would be her judges. In another minute their smiling,
flattering faces would be stern and implacable. She
would read mockery, malice, and icy contempt on those
faces, and then a perpetual, dawnless night would follow. No, I did not at the time understand it all as I do
now. All I could do was to suspect, to foresee, and to
grieve for the danger which threatened her and the
nature of which I only vaguely realised. But whatever
her secret might have been, it was amply expiated, if
any expiation was needed, by those sorrowful moments
which I witnessed and which I shall never forget.

But presently came the cheerful call to get ready to
leave; everyone was bustling about joyfully; laughter
and lively chatter was heard everywhere. Two minutes
later the terrace was deserted. Mrs. M—— refused to
go on the excursion, admitting at last that she was not
feeling well. But, thank God, they all went off. They
were all in a hurry to go, and there was no time to
worry her with expressions of regret, questions, and
all sorts of advice. A few remained at home. Her husband said something to her, she replied that she would
be all right very soon, that there was no need for him
to worry, that she did not think it necessary to lie
down, that she would go for a walk in the garden
alone . . . with me. Here she glanced at me. Nothing
could be more fortunate! I blushed with joy. A minute later we were on the way.

She walked along the same avenues, paths, and
tracks by which she had so recently returned from the

wood, instinctively remembering the way, her eyes
fixed on the ground, looking for something without
answering me and perhaps forgetting that I was walking beside her.

But when we almost reached the place where I had
picked up the letter and where the path came to an
end, Mrs. M—— suddenly stopped and in a weak
voice, faint with anguish, said that she felt worse and
was going home. But when she reached the garden
fence, she stopped again. She thought for a moment,
a despairing smile hovering on her lips and, utterly
worn out, exhausted, and ready to face whatever was
in store for her, silently retraced her steps, this time
even forgetting to warn me of her intention. . . .

I felt miserable and did not know what to do. We
went, or rather I brought her to the place where an
hour earlier I had heard the gallop of a horse and their
conversation. Here, near a shady elm tree, was a seat
hewn out of one huge piece of rock and overgrown
with ivy, wild jasmine and dog-rose. (The whole of the
little wood was covered with little bridges, arbours,
grottos, and similar surprises.) Mrs. M—— sat down
on the seat, glancing impassively at the beautiful view
that stretched before us. A minute later she opened
her book and sat staring at it motionless without turning the pages, without reading, and almost without
realising what she was doing. It was half past nine.
The sun had risen high and was sailing magnificently
over us across the deep, blue sky, as though melting
in its own fire. The haymakers had gone far away and
could scarcely be seen from our side of the river. End-
less furrows of mown grass crept inexorably after them,
and from time to time the faintly stirring breeze

wafted its fragrant exhalations to us. All around us we could hear the never-ceasing concert of those who "sow not, neither do they reap" but are as self-willed as the wind cleft by their sportive wings. It seemed as though at that very moment every flower and blade of grass was sending up wisps of sacrificial fragrance and saying to its creator: "Father, I am blessed and happy!" I glanced at the poor woman who alone was like a dead thing amidst all that joyous life: two big tears hung motionless on her eyelashes, wrung from her heart by sharp pain. It was in my power to bring back to life this poor, sinking heart and make her happy, only I did not know what to do, how to take the first step. I was in agony. A hundred times I was about to go up to her, and every time an uncontrollable feeling rooted me to the spot, and every time my face glowed like fire.

Suddenly I had a bright idea. A way had been found. I revived.

"Would you like me to pick you a bunch of flowers?" I exclaimed in such a joyous voice that Mrs. M—— suddenly raised her head and looked at me intently.

"Yes, do," she said at last in a weak voice, smiling faintly, and dropped her eyes on her book.

"They will probably mow the grass here, too, and there won't be any flowers left," I exclaimed, going joyfully off on my mission.

Soon I had picked my bunch of poor, simple flowers. I should have been ashamed to take it into a room, but how joyfully did my heart beat when I had picked it and tied it up! The dog-roses and the wild jasmine I found nearby. I knew there was a field of ripening rye not far away. I ran off there to pick some cornflowers. I mixed them up with the tall ears of rye,

choosing the ripest and most golden ones. Not far
from there I came across a whole bed of forget-me-
nots, and my bunch was beginning to take shape. A
little further in the field I found dark blue campanulas
and wild pinks and I ran down to the very bank of the
river for yellow water-lilies. At last, on my way back to
the seat I ran for a moment into the wood to get a
few bright green palmated maple leaves to put round
my bunch of flowers, and there I lighted upon a whole
family of pansies, and not far from them, luckily for
me, the fragrant scent of violets revealed the little
flowers hiding in the thick, lush grass and still covered
with glistening drops of dew. The bunch of flowers was
complete. I tied it with long thin grass which I twisted
into a string, and inside it I carefully placed the letter,
covering it with flowers so that it should be immediately noticeable if even the smallest attention was paid
to my bouquet.

I took it to Mrs. M——.

On the way I thought that the letter was still too
visible and I covered it a little more. On getting nearer,
I pressed it deeper into the flowers and, finally, when
I practically had approached the seat, I suddenly
pushed it so deeply inside the bunch of flowers that
nothing could be seen from outside. My cheeks were
positively aflame. I felt like burying my face in my
hands and running away at once, but she glanced at
my flowers as though she had completely forgotten
that I had gone to gather them for her. She stretched
out her hand mechanically, almost without looking,
took my present and immediately put it down on the
seat, as though I had given it to her for that purpose
and again dropped her eyes on her book. I felt like

crying at the failure of my plan. "If only my bunch of flowers were near her," I thought, "if only she would not forget it!" I lay down on the grass not far away, put my right arm under my head, and momentarily closed my eyes as though overcome by sleep. But I did not take my eyes off her and waited. . . .

Ten minutes passed. I thought she was getting paler and paler. . . . Suddenly a happy chance came to my aid.

It was a big, golden bee, which, luckily for me, was brought by a kindly breeze. At first it buzzed over my head and then flew up to Mrs. M——. She tried to wave it off once or twice, but, as though on purpose, the bee was getting more and more persistent. At last Mrs. M—— snatched up my flowers and waved them in front of her. At that moment the letter dropped out from among the flowers and fell straight on her open book. I started. For some time Mrs. M—— stared, bewildered, first at the book, then at the flowers in her hand and seemed unable to believe her own eyes. . . . Suddenly she coloured, flushed crimson, and glanced at me. But I had already anticipated her glance and closed my eyes tight, pretending to be asleep. Not for anything in the world would I have looked her straight in the face at that moment. My heart missed a beat and then leaped about like a little bird that has fallen in the clutches of a village boy. I cannot remember how long I lay with my eyes shut: two or three minutes perhaps. At last I plucked up courage and opened them. Mrs. M—— was greedily reading the letter, and I could see from her burning cheeks, her sparkling, tearful eyes, and her bright face, every feature of which was quivering with joyful emotion, that there was happiness in that letter and her sorrow was dispersed like smoke. My heart was seized by an agonisingly sweet feeling, and I found it difficult to go on pretending. . . .

I shall never forget that minute.

Suddenly, still far away from us, we heard voices:

"Natalie! Natalie!"

Mrs. M—— did not reply, but quickly got up from her seat, went up to me, and bent over me. I felt that she was looking straight into my face. My eyelashes trembled, but I controlled myself and did not open my eyes. I tried to breathe regularly and quietly, but the wild throbbing of my heart nearly choked me. Her burning breath scorched my cheeks. She bent more and more closely to my face as though wishing to test it. At last a kiss and tears fell on my hand, on the one that lay on my breast. She kissed it twice.

"Natalie! Natalie, where are you?" we heard again, but this time quite close.

"Coming!" said Mrs. M—— in her rich, silvery voice, but now choked and quivering with tears, and so quietly that only I could hear her. "Coming!"

But at that moment my heart at last betrayed me and seemed to send all my blood rushing to my face. At the same time a rapid, burning kiss scorched my lips. I cried out weakly, opened my eyes, but at once the gauze kerchief, which she had tied round my neck the day before, fell on my eyes, just as though she wished to screen me from the sun. An instant later she was no longer there. I only heard the faint sound of rapidly retreating steps. I was alone.

I pulled off the kerchief and covered it with kisses, beside myself with rapture. For a few minutes I was like one bereft of reason. Almost gasping for breath, leaning on the grass, I stared unconsciously and motionless before me, at the surrounding hills, covered with cornfields of different colours, at the river meandering round them and twisting for miles ahead, as far as the eye could see, between more hills and villages that gleamed like dots over the sunlit distance, at the blue, barely visible woods, which seemed to smoke on the edge of the burning sky, and a sort of sweet calm, inspired by the solemn silence of the picture, gradually brought peace to my troubled heart. I felt much better and I breathed more freely. But my whole soul seemed to be sweetly pining for something that was only vaguely perceived, as though by some insight into the future, by some foreboding. My fearful heart seemed to divine something, for it was faintly quivering with expectation. . . . Then suddenly my chest heaved and began to ache dully as though something had pierced it and tears, sweet tears gushed from my eyes. I covered my face with my hands and, trembling all over like a blade of grass, gave myself up freely to the first consciousness and revelation of my heart, the first still vague divination of my nature. The first period of my childhood was over from that moment.

When two hours later I returned home, I did not find Mrs. M——: she had left for Moscow with her husband because of some emergency. I never met her again.

ANCHOR BOOKS

FICTION

THE ANCHOR ANTHOLOGY OF SHORT FICTION OF THE SEVENTEENTH CENTURY—Charles C. Mish, ed., AC1

BANG THE DRUM SLOWLY—Mark Harris, A324

THE CASE OF COMRADE TULAYEV—Victor Serge, A349

COME BACK, DR. CALIGARI—Donald Barthelme, A470

THE COUNTRY OF THE POINTED FIRS—Sarah Orne Jewett, A26

DREAM OF THE RED CHAMBER—Chin Tsao Hseueh, A159

THE ENGLISH IN ENGLAND—Rudyard Kipling; Randall Jarrell, ed., A362

ENVY AND OTHER WORKS—Yuri Olesha; trans. by Andrew R. MacAndrew, A571

HALF-WAY TO THE MOON: New Writings from Russia—Patricia Blake and Max Hayward, eds., A483

HEAVEN'S MY DESTINATION—Thornton Wilder, A209

A HERO OF OUR TIME—Mihail Lermontov, A133

IN THE VERNACULAR: The English in India—Rudyard Kipling; Randall Jarrell, ed., A363

INFERNO, ALONE and Other Writings—August Strindberg, trans. by Evert Sprinchorn, A492c

THE LATE MATTIA PASCAL—by Luigi Pirandello, trans. by William Weaver, A479

LIFE OF LAZARILLO DE TORMES—W. S. Merwin, trans., A316

A MADMAN'S DEFENSE—August Strindberg, trans. by Evert Sprinchorn, A492b

A MAN OF THE PEOPLE—Chinua Achebe, A594

THE MASTERS—C. P. Snow, A162

POOR PEOPLE AND A LITTLE HERO—Fyodor Dostoevsky, trans. by David Magarshack, A619

REDBURN: HIS FIRST VOYAGE—Herman Melville, A118

THE SECRET AGENT—Joseph Conrad, A8

THE SHADOW-LINE AND TWO OTHER TALES—Joseph Conrad, A178

THE SON OF A SERVANT: The Story of the Evolution of a Human Being (1849–1867)—August Strindberg; trans. by Evert Sprinchorn, A492a

CLASSICS AND HUMANITIES